Praise for *Fifty Shames of Earl Grey*

"I'm laughing as much as I was when I read the original *Fifty Shades*."
—Alyssa Palmer, erotic romance author of *Prohibited Passion*

"I'm not telling you to buy *Fifty Shames of Earl Grey* because I'm banging the author. I'm telling you to buy *Fifty Shames of Earl Grey* AND I'm banging the author."
—Tiffany Reisz, author of the BDSM erotica series,
The Original Sinners

"Wickedly funny and irreverent. I laughed throughout the entire book and couldn't put it down. . . . Don't miss this book."
—Laurie London, author of the *Sweetblood*
paranormal romance series

"Hilarious. . . . A super fun read, like going to Six Flags with Zooey Deschanel."
—Kitty Glitter, author of *Wesley Crusher: Teenage F*** Machine*

Fifty Shames
of Earl Grey

Fifty Shames of Earl Grey

Fanny Merkin
(aka Andrew Shaffer)

Da Capo Press
A Member of the Perseus Books Group

Copyright © 2012 by Andrew Shaffer

Editorial production by *Marra*thon Production Services. www.marrathon.net

Design by Jane Raese

Library of Congress Cataloging-in-Publication Data is available for this book.
ISBN 978-0-306-82199-8 (paperback)
ISBN 978-0-306-82200-1 (e-book)

First Da Capo Press edition 2012

Published by Da Capo Press
A Member of the Perseus Books Group

www.dacapopress.com

Da Capo Press books are available at special discounts for bulk purchases in the U.S. by corporations, institutions, and other organizations. For more information, please contact the Special Markets Department at the Perseus Books Group, 2300 Chestnut Street, Suite 200, Philadelphia, PA, 19103, or call (800) 810-4145, ext. 5000, or e-mail special.markets@perseusbooks.com.

10 9 8 7 6

Chapter One

I GROWL WITH FRUSTRATION at my reflection in the mirror. My hair is fifty shades of messed up. Why is it so kinky and out of control? I need to stop sleeping with it wet. As I brush my long brown hair, the girl in the mirror with brown eyes too big for her head stares back at me. Wait . . . my eyes are blue! It dawns on me that I haven't been looking into the mirror—I've been staring at a poster of Kristen Stewart for five minutes. My own hair is fine.

The situation I'm in, however, is still fifty shades of messed up. My roommate, Kathleen, has the brown bottle flu. What a B. She was supposed to be the one interviewing this mega-corporate beefcake for *Boardroom Hotties* magazine. Since she's too busy throwing up buckets of puke into the toilet, I've been volunteered to do her dirty work. (The interview, not cleaning up her vomit.) I am mere weeks away from graduating from college with a liberal arts bachelor's degree. Instead of studying for my final exams, though, I'm about to ride my bike three and a half hours from Portland, Oregon, to downtown Seattle to meet with Earl Grey, the fabulously wealthy CEO of the Earl Grey Corporation. The interview can't be rescheduled, Kathleen says, because Mr.

Grey's time is precious and oh-so-valuable. Like mine isn't? As I said, my roommate is a total B.

Kathleen is sprawled out on the living room couch watching *16 and Pregnant*. This wouldn't be so bad if she was my age and in school, but she's old enough to be my mom. If they ever do a show called *Washed Up at 38*, I'm sure she'll be the first cast. She's a staff writer for *Boardroom Hotties*, a gig she treats as her own Rich Asshole dating service. None of the corporate executives she's profiled have proposed to her, but she has made sandwiches with quite a few of them. "You have to start somewhere," she always says. "Why not with peanut-butter-jelly time?" I don't know what's wrong with a good All-American HJ, but then again my experience with the opposite sex is almost nonexistent.

Kathleen looks up from her TV show and sees how annoyed I am with her. "I'm sorry, Anna. It took me months to get this interview. Please do this for me," she begs me with her raspy Christian Bale–as–Batman voice. Somebody smoked too many cigarettes last night.

"Of course I'll do it, Kathleen. You need to rest. Do you need any NyQuil?"

"Does it have alcohol in it?"

"Yes," I say.

"Then pour a shot into a glass with some Red Bull," she says. "And here—take my mini–disc recorder, and ask him these questions. I'll do the transcribing."

I can't believe I'm doing this! I take the mini–disc recorder and notebook from her and hop on my bicycle.

It's only after I'm peddling on the highway for a half hour that I remember her request for NyQuil and Red Bull. Oh, well. That B can get off her sick butt and mix her own drink.

⌒◯

The Earl Grey Corporation headquarters in downtown Seattle is a ginormous 175-story office building that juts into the cloudless sky like a steel erection. I walk through the glass doors and into the lobby, which is floor-to-ceiling glass and steel. This fascinates me to no end, because buildings back in Portland are made of grass and mud.

An attractive blonde behind the receptionist's desk smiles at me as I walk in. I assume she's the receptionist, because I can't think of any other reason she would be sitting behind the receptionist's desk. Unless maybe she's filling in for the real receptionist, who could be on her lunch break. But then I remember: it's almost two, and I doubt anyone takes their lunch breaks that late. So this must be the actual receptionist.

"I'm here to see Mr. Grey," I say. "My name is Anna Steal. I'm filling in for Kathleen Kraven."

"Just a moment, Miss Steal," the receptionist says, checking her computer. I wish I had borrowed one of Kathleen's suit jackets for the interview. Standing here in this big building in front of this professionally dressed woman, I feel naked in my Tommy hoodie and Victoria's Secret sweatpants with PINK written across the ass. The sweatpants aren't pink, though—they're gray. This always confuses me when I put them on, because shouldn't they say GRAY—on the backside? Maybe Victoria's secret is that she's colorblind.

The receptionist glances up from her computer. "Please sign in, Miss Steal," she says, pushing a clipboard with an attached pen across the desk to me. "You'll want to take the elevator to the ninetieth floor."

I stare at her blankly. We don't have elevators in Portland. "This will be my first elevator ride. How do they work, exactly?"

She smiles. "The elevator car that you ride in is suspended in a shaft by a steel rope, which is looped around a grooved pulley called a 'sheave.' An electric motor rotates the sheave, raising and lowering the elevator car."

"That's fascinating," I say. "Can I operate it myself?"

"Elevators are very simple to operate. Once you're inside, you just have to press the button that says 'ninety,'" she says as I sign in. There's a hint of sarcasm in her voice, but I let it slide. They're probably not used to dealing with hicks from Portland around here.

The receptionist hands me a security badge that reads VIRGIN. Is it that obvious? "How did you know—"

"That you're a first-time visitor here at the Earl Grey Corporation? Relax," she says, winking. "I was just as nervous as you were the first time I met Earl Grey."

I thank her and head toward the elevator. Two bald, muscular men dressed like secret service agents are standing guard, and one who looks exactly like Vin Diesel pushes the "up" arrow as I approach. Upon closer inspection, it *is* Vin Diesel. *Woah.* I step onto the elevator, push the button marked "90," and the magical box hurtles up toward Mr. Grey's office. It's like an amusement park ride, only it's free, you don't have to stand in line for two hours, and no one's thrown up all over the floor. Which makes me think of Kathleen again.

The elevator finally slows to a halt. The doors open and I'm in another lobby made of glass and steel. Is the whole building made with the same materials? Where did they ever find so much glass and steel? I begin to do what I always do when I'm thinking: pick my nose. Before I can shove my pinkie in too far, another attractive blonde greets me and guides me to a pleather beanbag chair. "Wait here, Miss Steal," she says coolly.

I sink down into the beanbag chair and watch the blonde leave down a hallway. Does Earl Grey employ any male receptionists? What a creep. I dig through my backpack and pull out Kathleen's notebook and glance over her questions. Who is this man I'm supposed to interview, this man whose last name is the same as the color of my sweatpants? Is that a sign? That B Kathleen didn't tell me anything about him, and I didn't think to ask. My brain is always going blank. This guy could be a hundred years old or five. Although they wouldn't let a five-year-old run a company the size of the Earl Grey Corporation, would they? Then I remember: they totally would. I saw it in a movie when I was little. *Richie Rich*, starring that cute boy from *Home Alone*. God, if I have to interview an effing kid for the next hour, I'm going to jump out the window right now! I can't contain my nervous energy. My leg starts twitching. I'd rather be alone, curled up in a ball in my bed, crying myself to sleep. Anything but about to interview some five-year-old billionaire.

Stop it, Anna, a voice says with a thick Jersey accent. It takes me a second to realize that it's my inner guidette. I can tell it's her, because when she talks inside my head there's this weird echoey sound. *There's no friggin' way he's five years old. Or a hundred. If he's being profiled in* Boardroom Hotties, *he's probably like every other CEO they lust after: late twenties or thirties and handsome in that geeky sort of way.* I breathe a sigh of relief, because I know my inner guidette is probably right.

The blonde returns. "Miss Steal?"

"Yes," I say, in a deeper voice than usual, trying to mask my crisis of confidence.

"Mr. Grey will see you in a few minutes. Would you like a refreshment while you wait? Coffee, soda, tea . . .?"

"Gravy," I say.

It's supposed to be a joke, but the woman nods and heads back down the corridor. A minute later, she returns with a clear pint glass filled with thick, brown gravy. Before I can ask for water instead, the office door connected to the lobby swings open and a handsome African American gentleman exits. Jay-Z!

Turning and pointing a finger back through the door, the rapper says, "Nine holes, this week." I assume he's talking about golf, but my mind starts to drift to thoughts of other holes. Jay-Z winks at me as he passes on his way to the elevator.

My phone buzzes—it's a text message from Beyoncé, warning me to keep my hands off her man. Whatever.

"Mr. Grey will see you now," the receptionist calls out to me from behind her desk. I pick up my backpack and notebook, and check my hoodie pocket for the mini–disc recorder. Still there. I leave the gravy and make my way slowly toward the open door. I should be back in Portland, studying for my finals so that I can graduate. Yet here I am, doing Kathleen's dirty work. I'm going to murder her, if Beyoncé doesn't kill me first.

I push the door open and trip over the hem of my sagging sweatpants in one swift, clumsy motion. As I career toward the floor, my body reflexively reverts to gymnast mode. I drop the backpack and notebook, throw my arms out straight, and roll into a cartwheel. With the momentum picked up from tripping, I complete three full cartwheels before landing on my feet—on Mr. Grey's desk! I am so embarrassed about my clumsiness that I close my eyes.

Wait. Someone is . . . clapping? I open my eyes and stare down at Mr. Grey and HOLY MOTHER EFFING SPARKLY VAMPIRES IS HE HOT.

Chapter Two

M ISS KRAVEN," the handsome CEO says, extending a long-fingered hand to me to assist me off his desk. I'd expected him to be British, but there's no trace of an English accent in his voice. "I'm Edward Cullen. I mean, 'Earl Grey.' Have a seat?"

He's young, he's sexy, he's tall—he's the total package. And no way is he five years old. He can't be more than thirty. He's dressed impeccably in a tailored gray suit, pressed white dress shirt, and a black tie with smiley faces on it. With his tousled brown hair and brilliant gray eyes, he's the kind of guy you want to write fanfic about.

"Well, um," I say, accepting his hand and stepping off the desk. I blink my eyes rapidly as we touch; either his touch is electric, or I just had a seizure. When I'm back on my feet on the floor I excuse myself to pick up my notebook and backpack, and then return to sit down across from him.

"Miss Kraven had an emergency come up at the last minute. She sent me instead."

"And your name is . . .?"

"Anna Steal. Miss Kraven and I are roommates."

"Mmmm-hmmmm," he says.

I pull the mini—disc recorder out of my pocket and set it up. Mr. Grey watches me with an amused look on his face. He's probably wondering why I'm using technology that was obsolete the day it rolled off the production line. I have the same question. The only thing I know is that Kathleen is obsessed with vintage stuff. I mean, her favorite band is Nirvana.

"Sorry," I mutter. "I'm trying to figure out how to turn this thing on . . ."

"It's okay. I like to watch," he says with a malicious smile.

"Can I record our conversation? It's for Kathleen."

"I don't mind if you tape us," he says. The way he says "us" sends shivers up my spine. Is he hitting on me? I'm not used to this kind of attention from a man. I've never been the "hot girl"; my body is unremarkable in just about every way, from my too-narrow hips to my B-cups.

"Kathleen told you what this interview was about, right?" I say.

"I've never spoken with her, but my assistant has informed me it's for some sort of business magazine."

"Um, yeah," I say, finally figuring out how to turn on the mini—disc recorder. If he doesn't know what kind of magazine it is, I'm not going to be the one to explain it to him. "So, she gave me a list of questions to ask you."

He stares at me unwaveringly with his gray eyes. "And . . .?"

No small talk, apparently. I read the first question word for word out of the notebook. "You're young and have achieved a lot in your business career, more than most people will achieve in their lifetimes. What's the secret of your success?"

He smiles. "The most important part of my business is the people I employ and the people my company does business with. I spend a lot of time getting to know people and judging them. I inspire them, incentivize them, and reward them. I employ over a billion people in my vast empire, and I interviewed every one of them myself. They're all outstanding human beings. So, in short, my success has everything to do with the people I surround myself with."

"Couldn't it be luck?" This isn't something Kathleen wrote down, but I have to go off script—he seems so arrogant and sure of himself. I want to throw him off guard. This is going to be the best damn puff piece that has ever run in *Boardroom Hotties*.

"Luck is for gamblers, Miss Steal. I don't gamble."

"Never? You've never, say, played the lottery?"

"Never," he says. "I don't take chances."

"Not even, like, a one dollar scratch-off ticket?"

"Never. I just can't take that kind of chance. If the ticket's not a winner, I'm left with a little scrap of paper with silver dust all over my quarter. And sometimes that silvery stuff gets on your fingers and it's a bitch to clean off."

"So you have bought scratch-off lottery tickets!"

He sighs. "Off the record? My mother was a gambling addict, Miss Steal. She gave me used scratch-off lottery tickets instead of toys to play with as a child. So I don't take chances."

"Not even for a dollar," I mutter.

"Not even for a dollar," he says, boring through my skull with his gray eyes.

I feel my heartbeat quickening. Everything he says makes me want to make sandwiches with him, even the part about playing with lottery tickets as a kid. Is it because he's so good looking? Is it because of his incredibly long fingers? Or his tousled hair? Or his incredibly long fingers?

"Do you ever rest?" I ask. "How do you unwind?"

"I have hobbies," he says, smirking. "Physical pursuits: base jumping, hang gliding, underwater basket weaving. I also enjoy intellectual activities, like board games."

"Monopoly, I presume," I say.

"Of course," he says. "But I also take pleasure in a good game of Trivial . . . Pursuit."

Gulp.

He's so attractive and long fingered that I find it hard to concentrate on asking the questions Kathleen has written down for me. I force myself to look at the page and read another one. "The Earl Grey Corporation has quite the diversified portfolio of businesses, from manufacturing to natural resources to Internet startups. Why not focus exclusively on the technology sector, like every other billionaire your age?"

He sighs. "I'm not like other people. I don't do what everyone else does," he says, "in business or in the bedroom."

Most people sleep or watch TV or read books in bedrooms. What could he be talking about?

"Do you have a philosophy of business?" I ask.

"No man is an island," he says. "Islands are made of dirt and rocks and trees. I don't know any people made of such things. Therefore, people are not islands."

Wow. Was this hot guy a philosophy major in college? He's nothing like the burnouts I know who sit around contemplating their navels and smoking grass. My skin feels flushed. I've never been in the presence of such a smart, attractive man before, except for the time President Obama gave a speech at our school and recited the name of every state (including capitals) in alphabetical order, entirely from memory.

"Your name is quite distinctive. Are you an English earl, by any chance?" I ask.

He shakes his head. "If I was, do you think I would have ended up in foster care in the United States? Plus, look at my perfect teeth."

"Point taken," I say. Since he brought it up, I move on to the next question, which is related. "How did being abandoned by your parents affect your business career?" As soon as I read the question, I feel like an even bigger idiot than I usually do. Why can't Kathleen be here doing this? Oh, yeah—she's at home getting sick off NyQuil–Red Bull bombs. In other words, a typical Tuesday for her.

"I didn't have a conventional upbringing. That's public knowledge. How has it affected my business career? I honestly don't know." Yikes. He's no longer smiling.

"Have you sacrificed having a wife and family for the sake of your career?"

"No, but I have sacrificed many the virgin," he says, smirking again. His mood changes as often as my mom changes husbands.

"Are you gay?" Another stupid question that Kathleen has written down!

A smile spreads on Mr. Grey's face. "Am I gay? No, Miss Steal. I'm not gay. I'm quite the opposite, in fact."

"What's the opposite of gay?"

"Sad," he says. "You meant 'gay' as in 'happy,' right?"

I take another look at the notebook. "It doesn't say here, Mr. Grey. It just says, 'gay.'"

"What kind of questions are these, exactly?"

"They're Kathleen's," I say sheepishly.

"Do you work with her at this business magazine?"

I shake my head and blush. "No. I'm a senior at Washington State, but my major is English, not journalism. This is the first interview I've ever conducted."

"I see," he says, rubbing his chin thoughtfully. Oh, how I'd like him to rub my—

The intercom on his desk rings, and he answers it. "Supermodel Jezebel Luscious is on the line, Mr. Grey," the receptionist says.

"Tell her to wait. I'm not finished with this meeting," he says, putting the world's most beautiful woman on hold—for me.

"Okay, Mr. Grey," the receptionist says. "Can you ask Miss Steal if she would like her gravy brought into your office? She left her glass in the lobby."

Earl cocks an eyebrow at me quizzically.

I shake my head.

"That won't be necessary," he says. "If she gets thirsty, I'm sure we can find something for her to drink in here."

He smiles villainously and hangs up the speakerphone. "Pardon the interruption. Where were we?"

"I think I've asked you all the questions Kathleen had."

"I see. Then perhaps you can answer some of my questions."

"I'm not that interesting, Mr. Grey."

"I'll be the judge of that," he says. "When do you graduate?"

"A couple of weeks."

"And afterward, what are your plans?"

"I don't have any. I was thinking something in publishing." I haven't put much thought into my future yet. I've only had four years to contemplate it.

"The Earl Grey Corporation owns several publishing houses. I can set you up with an interview at one of them," he says.

"Um, thanks," I say. "But I don't know if I'm someone you want on your team."

"Why not?"

"Nevermind," I say. I'm nothing like the blonde Barbies he has working for him. Can't he see that I'm the kind of girl who wears sweatpants to interview billionaires? I have to get out of his office before I make an even bigger fool of myself.

"Would you like a tour of the building? Perhaps a peek inside my secret sex dungeon?" he asks.

"Can't," I say, gathering up my things and turning the mini—disc recorder off. "I've got to work this evening. Thanks for the interview."

He extends his right hand. "The pleasure was all on this end," he says, smiling. I shake his hand, and feel the jolt of electricity again from him. He laughs and raises his hand to show me the joy-buzzer in his palm. What a prankster! "Good day, Miss Steal."

"Good day to you, Mr. Grey," I say, leaving.

Chapter Three

I SHARE A DUPLEX apartment in Portland with Kathleen. Her parents bought it for her when she started college over twenty years ago, and, as far as I know, they still think she's going to school. Kathleen says she's "taking a break." Although I have to put up with her drunken antics, the duplex has at least saved me the indignity of living in cheap student housing. As I pull my bike into our driveway, I sigh inwardly. Kathleen is going to want the deets on this handsome young CEO. I'll give her the mini–disc recording, but the stuff about him practically making love to me with his eyeballs for an hour? I'll keep that to myself.

As I step through the door, she launches herself off the couch and bounds toward me, tackling me to the ground and licking my face. She's like a 135-pound puppy sometimes, I swear. Maybe 140-pounds, since the SpaghettiOs and alcohol fad diet she's been on for the past three weeks seems to be working in reverse. I shrug her off, and we both stand up.

"I was worried about you," she says.

"Why?" I ask. *Because you sent me to Grandma's house when you knew the whole time there was a big bad wolf?*

"I was worried you wouldn't find Seattle. I know how you get lost on your way to the bathroom sometimes." She's talking about the time I squatted and peed in the kitchen. It was only that one time, and I was on shrooms.

"Well, I didn't get lost," I say, pulling the mini—disc recorder out and tossing it to her. We sit down on the couch. Kathleen turns the volume down on the *16 and Pregnant* marathon she's been caught up in. Isn't there something better on, like *Jersey Shore*?

"So, spill the beans," she says. "What was the infamous Mr. Earl Grey like?"

"You didn't tell me he would be so young," I say. "How old is he?"

"Twenty-seven."

"He's a nice guy. Like Mark Zuckerberg, only less autistic," I say. "He wears a suit, but he also has a peculiar sense of humor."

"Just tell me one thing: Is he straight? Did he flirt with you?"

"Oh, I don't know if I'm the kind of girl he'd be interested in," I say. "Just going by his secretaries, he's into tall, statuesque blondes."

"My hair is blond," Kathleen says. "And I can act like a statue." She purses her lips and holds her breath. I have to admit she does kind of look like a statue, what with the gray pallor of her skin and empty look in her eyes.

"How are you feeling?" I ask her.

"Better," Kathleen says, relaxing her body.

"Good," I say. "I have to leave for work."

"I can't believe you're working tonight. Don't you have finals to study for?"

Yes, I have finals to study for—that's what I was supposed to be doing all day long until it was time for me to go to work. I stare at her incredulously.

"Sorry, forget I asked," Kathleen says dismissively. "Do you want to do body shots before you go? I picked up some fresh limes . . ."

"Sounds tempting," I say. "But I'm going to be late enough as it is."

"Okay, your loss," she says. "Laters."

I'm glad to get to work, because it gives me a chance to do something besides daydream about Earl Grey. Walmart is the first and only job I've ever had. I've worked there all four years that I've been going to Washington State. Once I graduate, I'm going to start looking for a "real" job. I don't have anything lined up yet, but I'm not one to worry. In this economy, it shouldn't be too hard for a fresh college graduate to find a new job.

"I'm so happy you made it in today," my boss says as I slip on my blue smock in the employee break room. It's nearly summer, so of course my boss is happy to see me—we're so busy, what with everyone buying new grills for the summer. Doesn't anyone ever save their grill from one year to the next? Not in America, I guess.

"Sorry I'm late," I say.

"I'm just glad you're here. You know that, Anna—I'm always happy to see a full set of teeth around here."

I smile.

"Anyway," he continues, "someone dropped a massive load in the women's restroom and I need you to clean it up. It's the biggest damn thing I've ever seen come out of another human being."

I head to the women's restroom with a plunger and a pair of gardening shears, and I'm soon lost in my task. Earl Grey is the furthest thing from my mind.

The rest of the week I split my time working at Walmart and studying for my exams. Any free time I have I spend fantasizing about "interning" for Earl Grey. And by "interning," I mean doing two-person pushups with him. Kathleen transcribes the interview and works on her profile of him for *Boardroom Hotties*. She thanks me for conducting the interview for her and "taking one for the team." Oh, she has no idea how much I'd like to "take one" for the team.

On Wednesday, I call my mom. She lives in Florida with her sixth husband, some schlub whose name I can never remember. He reminds me of Louis CK, only without a sense of humor. They live in a nudist colony. I drove cross-country and visited them once, which was one time too many.

"How are classes going, Anna?"

"Okay, I guess," I say distantly.

"Anna? You sound like you've fallen in love with a mysterious older man."

"Yeah, right," I lie. "Like that would ever happen to me."

"Honey, you need to put yourself out there. You've never had a boyfriend. Or a girlfriend. Or a friend with benefits."

"Thanks for reminding me, Mom."

"I'm just saying, there's nothing wrong with having a little fun," she says. Maybe she's right. Who knows more about love and romance than someone who's on her sixth marriage?

After we finish talking, I call my dad. He doesn't like to talk on the phone, but I like to call and bug him anyway. After fifteen minutes of me blabbing my mouth off and him grunting awkwardly, I realize that I haven't called my dad—I dialed the wrong number, and some creepy guy is making a sandwich on the other end of the line. I hang up immediately. I'll call my dad another day; I need a shower.

I spend the rest of the night doing schoolwork. After striking a match and lighting a candle, I sit down at my desk with my quill pen and parchment to write an essay for my ethics class on the legalities of fan fiction. When I finish, it's one in the morning. I blow out my candle and crash on my bed, where I fall asleep to images of Earl Grey's gray eyes watching over me . . .

On Friday night, the doorbell rings as I'm studying and Kathleen is watching *Wall Street*. I answer the door. It's my best ethnic friend, Jin!

"Come in," I say, hugging him.

Jin and I have been friends since we were freshmen, though we've never dated. He's graduating this year as well. He's a communications major, but no one is really sure what that qualifies him to do after college. Like me, he's clueless about the real world.

He's holding a forty-ounce bottle of Olde English. "Good news," he says. "I've been promoted to forum moderator at PonyExpression.net."

When he's not in school or doing homework, Jin spends his free time reading and writing *My Little Pony* fanfic. He's deep into the "brony" scene. Who knew that there were so many male fans of *My Little Pony: Friendship Is Magic?* I never thought his obsession would amount to anything, but it sounds like I've been proven wrong. "Congratulations," I say, hugging him again. "How much will you be getting paid?"

He clears his throat. "It's, uh, peanuts," he says.

At least his parents are still footing his bills while he's in college. "Oh," I say. "Well. You can eat peanuts, after you shell them. Unless they're already shelled. Then you can just eat them."

Kathleen flashes Jin a thumbs-up from the couch. She hasn't been feeling well again, but what else is new.

"Anyway, I brought us some of the finest malt liquor to celebrate, bitches," he says. He's always calling Kathleen and me "bitches," but we all know that Kathleen's the only B in the duplex.

Although Jin and I are just friends, I'm pretty sure he wants us to be "more" than friends. I don't see him that way—he's more like a brother from another mother. He's tried to kiss me on more than one occasion, but I've always deflected his advances. Both my mom and Kathleen tease me about not having a sexual bone in my body, but that's not true—there's one bone I'd like to have in my body, and it's attached to Mr. Earl Grey . . .

Jin unscrews the cap off the Olde English and pours the beer into three red plastic Solo cups. As he does this, I notice his tanned skin, neatly cropped dark hair, and bulging muscles. He looks up at me, grinning. I smile back, weakly, wondering if he'll ever stop trying to put his grabby hands on me. Probably not—Jin is the third wheel on this Anna Steal–Earl Grey bicycle built for two.

Chapter Four

I'M WORKING a full eight-hour shift at Walmart on Saturday. My boss assigns me to the cash registers all day. I can't think of any better motivation for passing my final exams and graduating than the thought of working here for the rest of my life.

By the fourth hour of scanning and bagging diapers and cigarettes, I'm in such a daze that I don't realize the customer in front of me is none other than Earl Grey! He is dressed in a gray velour sweat suit that compliments his eyes. I didn't think it was possible for him to look any yummier than he did in his business suit, but damn.

"Hello, Miss Steal," he says, gazing at me gazingly with his gazing gray eyes.

"Mr. Grey!"

He slides a Nickelback CD toward me, which I scan. "I happened to be in the area and here you are," he says. "What a pleasant surprise."

"Did you, um, find everything that you were looking for today?" I mutter, bagging the CD. Earl Grey is smiling again like the big bad wolf who wants to eat me. And boy, do I want him to eat my—

"Actually, no," he says, cutting off my internal mono-
logue. "There were a few things I couldn't find on my own.
Could you help me out?" His voice is cool and gritty like a
Wendy's Frosty, and my mind momentarily goes blank.

I shake my head to gather my thoughts. Like a magic eight
ball, a thought pops up for me. "Signs point to yes," I say.

"Excuse me?"

"I mean, yes. Of course I can help you."

There's a line of fifteen people behind him, but how can
I resist that voice? I turn my lane's light off. I can hear
groans from the customers who have been waiting in line,
but there are three other cashiers working. There's only
one Earl Grey.

He hands me his shopping list and I lead him through
the store in search of the items. *Duct tape? Plastic wrap? A hack-
saw?* Who is this guy, Dexter? I lead him toward the aisle
with tape, and it takes all of my available mental capacity to
concentrate on walking. *Left foot, right foot, left foot . . . right foot?*

"Shoot, we forgot your CD," I say.

He waves a hand. "I have ten copies of it at home anyway," he says. This guy throws money around like a monkey
throws crap.

"So what are you doing here in Portland? Business?" I
ask him.

"Pleasure," he says. I feel my womb instinctively heat up,
preparing itself to incubate our babies.

I stop. "Here's the aisle with tape."

"Thank you, Miss Steal," he says. He picks up the most

expensive brand, which runs $3.99 a roll. This guy is a total baller.

"You like to live large," I say.

"Does that impress you, Miss Steal?"

I blush. "I've never known anyone with so much money," I say. "That came out totally wrong. Sorry."

"It's okay," he says, grinning. "It's true, isn't it?"

"What?"

"That I have a lot of money."

I nod. "Can I ask what you're doing at Walmart? I mean, you can afford to shop anywhere."

He laughs. "Oh, Miss Steal. I love your honesty. It's so refreshing. Usually the only women I meet are sycophantic to the point of revulsion. Not you."

"I'll take that as a compliment," I say.

"As you should. Now to answer your question: Why would one of the world's wealthiest men shop at Walmart? For one thing, Walmart has the lowest prices around."

I don't want to offend him, but I might as well say what I'm thinking. "It's just a little . . . low class. If I had your money, I'd shop at Target."

"I'm not your average billionaire," he says.

I smile. "No, you're certainly not, Mr. Grey."

He flashes that wicked smile of his at me. "Take your finger out of your nose, Miss Steal."

"Sorry," I say, pulling my finger out.

"It's okay," Earl says. "Care to join me for coffee?"

My heart pounds inside my chest, pumping blood to my

organs. Because that's what hearts do. Is Earl Grey asking me out on a date? "When?"

"Now," he says.

"My shift isn't over until six," I say glumly.

"Hold on," he says. He pulls a BlackBerry from his pants pocket and taps on it. It buzzes, and he taps on it again before stashing it away. "I think you can take the rest of the afternoon off."

"We're so busy on Saturdays. I really can't—my boss would kill me," I say.

"I'm your boss now, Miss Steal."

"What do you mean?"

There's that smile again, the one with all those teeth. "I just bought Walmart," he says.

"The whole company? Just so I could take the afternoon off to get coffee with you?"

"Yes, Miss Steal," he says. "Now take off that ugly blue smock and let's go."

He's so confident and forceful, unlike any boyfriend I've ever had. Well, he's not my boyfriend, and I haven't ever had a boyfriend, but you know what I mean, right? He's like a really rich caveman. *Me. Want. Anna!*

"What about your shopping list?" I ask.

"Forget it. I'll have one of my assistants do my shopping."

"Um—Mr. Grey—I don't know what to say."

"Just say 'yes.'" He smiles at me again with that smiling smile of his, all his teeth in a straight line. How I'd like to run my tongue along those teeth . . .

"Yes! Yes, yes, yes—oh yes, Mr. Grey!" I scream, throwing my smock off. It hits a customer riding a Rascal scooter in the face, and she crashes into a display of Katy Perry perfume. I pull my shirt over my nose to avoid choking on the vapors from the spilled perfume; Walmart suddenly smells like a prosti-tot pageant. Earl takes my hand in his and leads me out of the store before the hazmat team arrives.

Chapter Five

Earl grey has a helicopter waiting for us in the Walmart parking lot. "Where's the pilot?" I ask.

"Right here, baby," he says, pointing two thumbs toward his chest. For the first time since he showed up in my checkout lane, I let my eyes wander the full length of his body. The bulge running down the side of his pants leg is quite noticeable. Then I notice a similar bulge running down the side of his other pants leg. Either he has a banana in each pocket, or he's *really* happy to see me.

We step into the helicopter's cockpit and he takes control of the controls like the controlling man he is. He flashes me that smile again, the one that makes me soak my sweatpants.

"I've never been in a helicopter before," I say as the helicopter blades start spinning overhead. "Heck, I've never even flown on an airplane. This is so exciting, Mr. Grey."

"You haven't seen anything yet, Anna," he says. It's the first time he's called me by my first name. *Swoon.* "Do you know what the Mile High Club is?"

I shake my head. "Is that some sort of country club for aviators?"

"Sort of," he says, smirking.

Before I know it, we're off the ground and soaring above the parking lot. The people are so small from this height; they look like ants (although they're wearing clothes and have two legs instead of six). This is amazing. I'm in a helicopter with Earl Grey, the most handsomest man on the planet. And now he's the most handsomest man in the air! I peer into the distance, and can see the Space Needle in faraway Seattle jutting above the skyline. We're up so high, and the sun is so bright—

"Earl!" I shout.

"What!" he shouts back, over the roar of the helicopter's massive blades.

"Watch out for the sun!"

"What!"

"I said, WATCH OUT FOR THE SUN!"

He shoots me a puzzled look.

"What? I'm not wearing sunscreen," I say.

He shakes his head.

"Nevermind," I mutter. He probably knows how close to the sun we can fly without getting burned. I hope.

As we begin our descent, I get butterflies in my stomach. I close my mouth, because I don't want to pull a Kathleen and spew chunks all over Earl. He lands the helicopter at the Starbucks across the street from Walmart.

"We're here," Earl says wickedly. You might not think someone can say "we're here" wickedly, but if you heard Earl say it, you would totes agree. He says everything wickedly.

We step out of the helicopter and he leads me, hand in hand, into the Starbucks. He's not wearing his joy-buzzer, but his touch is still electric. I gaze into his gazing eyes gazingly like a gazelle gazing into another gazelle's gazing gaze. WHAM!

The next thing I know, I'm on my back on the concrete. He reaches a hand out to help me up. "Are you okay, baby?"

"I think so," I say as he pulls me back to my feet. *I was just gazing into your eyes too gazingly, and ran into the door. Stupid Anna!*

Earl opens the door for me, and this time I walk through it instead of into it. "Grab us a table and I'll grab the drinks," he says. Another smirk! The only time I've seen someone smile this much was the time Kathleen and I did E. "What would you like?"

"Tea, please."

"No coffee?"

"I drink coffee sometimes, but Starbucks' coffee tastes like burnt ass," I say.

"Actually, it tastes *nothing* like burnt ass, Anna."

"And how would you know what burnt ass tastes like?"

He laughs. "That's for me to know . . . and you to find out."

I'm not sure I want to find out, but whatever.

He starts toward the counter, then stops. "I didn't ask you what kind of tea you wanted," he says to me.

"Isn't it obvious?" I say. Now it's my turn to smirk. "Earl Grey. Hot."

"Do you take milk or sugar with that?" he asks, grinning.

I've lost track of what he's trying to hint at. I think he's literally asking if I want milk or sugar for my tea, but he could very well be asking if I want them for my ass. "No thanks," I say.

He heads off toward the register as I sit down at an empty table. Now safely seated, I no longer have to worry about walking into any doors as I ogle him. I watch him order, and he orders wickedly. He is tall, muscular, and has the kind of shoulders you want to jump on and take a piggyback ride on. I watch as he pulls his credit card out of his wallet using his long fingers, which I swear have to be longer than his forearms.

A few minutes later, he brings my Earl Grey tea and his coffee to our table. *Our* table! I can't believe I'm already thinking about us as a couple. What would our babies look like? Would they have long fingers too?

"Your tea, Anna," he says. "If I may be so bold to ask: Why Earl Grey?"

I shake my head. "I like my tea like I like my men," I say. *Named Earl Grey.* But I realize that might be too forward, so instead I say, "Black."

He raises an eyebrow.

"I mean, not that I exclusively like black men," I say. "I like other kinds of tea. And men."

"Have you ever tasted . . . white tea, Anna?"

Oh my. "I've never heard of it," I say.

"White tea is a lightly oxidized tea grown and harvested almost exclusively in China, primarily in the Fujian province," he says. "White tea comes from the delicate buds and younger leaves of the Chinese *Camellia sinensis* plant. These buds and leaves are allowed to wither in natural sunlight before they are lightly processed to prevent oxidation."

Wow. "Where does the name 'white tea' come from?"

"It derives from the fine silvery-white hairs on the unopened buds of the tea plant, which gives the plant a whitish appearance," he says, sipping his coffee.

"How do you know all of this?"

He pulls his BlackBerry out, opens an app, and pushes the device across the table to me. A web page is open to the "White tea" entry at Wikipedia. I read a few lines, and realize he just quoted the article word for word to me. "You copied Wikipedia! Even I know not to do that," I say. "My professors are always warning us about what an unreliable source that is."

"Your professors are idiots, Anna."

"So you weren't just reciting this article word for word?"

"Who do you think wrote the article, Anna?"

Woah. This guy writes for the Internet!

Earl takes the BlackBerry from me and stashes it back into his velour sweatpants pocket. He sips his coffee.

"Why did you ask me out, Mr. Grey? I don't think I'm your type of girl."

He cocks an eyebrow. "And how would you know my 'type,' Anna?"

I shrug. "I saw the kind of girls you hire: tall, blond hair, well dressed."

"So, based on a couple of receptionists who happen to look a certain way, out of the billion employees who work for me, you think you know my type?"

"I may have made a generalization there," I admit.

"You shouldn't be so quick to jump to conclusions," he says. "For instance, if I had assumed Jin was your boyfriend, I may not have asked you out today."

"How do you know about Jin?"

"I had your duplex outfitted with a surveillance system," Earl says.

Gulp.

"He's just a friend," I say. "We've never dated or anything."

"That's good to know," Earl says.

I sip my tea. Earl pulls a banana out of his pocket and peels it with his long fingers. "Want some?"

"No thank you," I say. *So we're down to just one banana in his pants.*

"Do I intimidate you, Anna?" he says.

"Why do you ask?"

"Because you seem nervous around me. You sound much more relaxed on the surveillance tapes I've watched."

I sigh heavily. "Yes, I'm a little nervous. I've never had a boyfriend, let alone a billionaire CEO stalker flying me around in his private helicopter and holding my hand and buying me tea."

"You're a mystery to me, baby," he says, biting the tip off the banana.

I blush. "Oh, stop."

"No, it's true," he says. "I have no idea what's going on inside that pretty little head of yours . . ."

"To be honest, I have no idea either," I say, looking down at the table to avoid his powerful gaze. "Most times, my mind is just an ongoing, present-tense, first-person monologue. It's like I'm writing a novel, constantly, but only in my brain. A really bad novel."

"Do you have any siblings?"

"No," I say.

"I knew that," he says. "We're both only children. Are your parents still together?"

"No, they're—"

"Divorced?" he says, finishing my sentence. "I knew that as well."

I eye him suspiciously. "You're a strange man, Mr. Grey."

"You have no idea," he says, finishing his banana off.

"Then why play twenty questions?"

"You interviewed me. I don't think I finished . . . probing you," Earl says, sipping his coffee.

"Probe away," I say, deliberately trying to shock the mighty Earl Grey. I succeed, because he accidentally spits his coffee out all over my face. *Oh my.*

"Sorry," he says, using a napkin to wipe me down. "You ready to get out of here?"

"Sure," I say.

He takes me by the hand and we leave Starbucks together. Are we going steady? This is all happening so fast! I ask him if he has a girlfriend.

"I'm not a 'girlfriend' kind of guy," he says.

Okay, so he's not a "girlfriend" kind of guy. And he's not gay. Or is he? He said he wasn't gay as in "happy," but he never explicitly said anything about not being homosexual. I'm trying to decode what he means, but the words keep bouncing around in my head like a broken magic eight ball, the answer never surfacing.

I step onto the sidewalk and trip over a homeless guy, flying headfirst into the street. Damn my clumsiness!

"Look out, Anna!" Earl screams. He pulls me back with both hands just as a hipster on a unicycle zips by, narrowly missing me by inches.

One minute I was walking along, happy to be alive—and the next, my life was flashing before my eyes. I'm not that interesting, so the slideshow of my life was painfully dull and mercifully short, but still. I was almost crushed to death by a hipster with a twirly mustache. Now Earl Grey is cradling me in his arms, and I feel like I've been born again. Like I have a second chance at life. I sniff him, and inhale his manly scent: Coconut Lime Breeze body wash from Bath & Body Works' Signature Collection. It retails for $12.50. This guy sure knows his body washes.

"My God, Anna," he says. "I almost lost you." He has me in his powerful grip. I've never felt this safe before.

"Never let go," I say, looking into his beautiful gray eyes.

"That could be problematic," he says. "I'll have to let you go at some point. What if I have to pee? What if you have to pee?"

"I don't care," I say.

"What if I have an important business meeting, and I'm holding you and we're both covered in urine?"

I start to cry. "You're right," I say, turning my face away from his gaze. "Nothing lasts forever." *Not even this perfect moment . . .*

"Um, excuse me? Could you guys get off me, please?" the homeless guy underneath us says. We stand up, and Earl hands him a hundred-thousand-dollar bill as an apology. The man scampers off, as homeless people are wont to do.

"That was so kind of you, Mr. Grey," I say.

"I can be kind . . . when I want to be." That wickedness is lurking just behind every word he says.

I want him to save me from another hipster, to grab ahold of me, to kiss me. *Kiss me, you arrogant man!* But there are no other unicycling hipsters for me to throw myself in front of, no more homeless people to trip over.

"Anna, stay away from me," Earl says, turning his back to me. *What? Why is he saying this?* He begins walking away, and then looks over his shoulder.

"I can be kind, but I can also be very, very cruel," he says.

"I don't care," I say.

"Anna . . ." He pauses. "Good luck with your life." He steps into his helicopter and flies away.

Tears are now streaming down my face. I guess I'm walking the fifty yards back to the Walmart parking lot.

Chapter Six

MY BOSS DIDN'T NOTICE I'd left work, so I finish out my shift. When I get home early in the evening, Kathleen is parked on the couch as usual. This time she's watching *Pretty Woman*.

"What's wrong, Anna?"

I try to walk swiftly past her to my room, but she throws the TV remote at my head, knocking me to the ground. "Ow," I say, getting back up.

"Answer me," she says. "Why have you been crying?"

"No reason," I mutter.

"It was *him*, wasn't it?"

I shake my head. "I don't know who you're talking about."

"Yes you do," she says. "Mr. Long Fingers. Mr. Womb-Ticklers."

I sigh. "Fine. Yes. I was at work, and he showed up. Just out of the blue. And he bought the company, and now he's my boss. At least I think he is? It's a little confusing. Anyway, we went on a romantic helicopter ride to Starbucks, and he knows so much about tea, and . . ."

"And what?"

"He saved me from some stupid *Portlandia* hipster on a unicycle."

"And that's it?" she says.

"Then he just told me off, like none of it meant anything to him."

"What a jerk-faced jerk-face!"

"I know."

"You're too good for him," Kathleen says.

I laugh. "Too good for Mr. Earl Grey? Please, girl."

"No, really," she says. "You're hot property. I'd do you."

"I think you did once," I say.

"Oh yeah."

"Anyway, I need to study," I say, leaving Kathleen to her movie. I open my door . . . and find the handsomest man in the whole world, Earl Grey, sitting on my bed!

"What are you doing here?" I say. What a creeper!

"I could ask you the same thing," he says.

"I live here," I say.

"I bought the duplex from Kathleen's parents this afternoon," he says. "I'm your landlord now. So technically I live here too." He pauses. "I heard what you said in the living room."

"I knew you would."

"I'm sorry," he says. "I'm not used to getting close to women I like."

Aha! So he *does* like women.

"Here," he says, handing me a package covered in Christmas wrapping paper.

"It's not Christmas," I say.

"It's the only wrapping paper my assistant could find," he says. "Don't worry—I've already fired her for it."

"Which assistant? One of your Barbie dolls?"

He looks at me, confused for a moment, and then says, "Now that you say that, I'm not entirely sure which assistant it was. I'll fire them all when I return to Seattle, just to be sure."

What a people person, my inner guidette whispers. I tell her to shove it. I take the present from him and begin tearing into it. "I'm supposed to be studying for my exams," I say.

"Not anymore," he says, smiling that wicked smile.

"What do you mean . . .?"

"I mean, I bought Washington State University," he says.

"But it's a public university!"

"Not anymore," he says, laughing.

The nerve of this insane, handsome man!

"You don't have to take your tests—classes are canceled. Everyone will graduate with honors."

Gulp.

"Finish opening the present, Anna."

"Okay," I say, peeling the last of the wrapping paper off to reveal a hardcover book covered in cloth. I'm too young to remember a time when print books were "a thing," but Kathleen has shelves full of them. I open it to the title page: *A Shore Thing* by Nicole "Snooki" Polizzi.

"It's Snooki's debut novel. This is a first printing," Earl says.

"How did you know I'm a *Jersey Shore* fan?"

"Let's just say I had a hunch," he says, glancing around the room at the half-dozen *Jersey Shore* posters plastered on the walls.

"This book is worth a fortune," I say. "I can't accept it."
"You have to," he says. "Please."

It's too much. I feel overwhelmed. First, he buys Wal-mart. Then, he buys my duplex. And then my school. And now, this . . . The book is over the line. I feel like he's trying to buy *me*.

I toss the book at him, and he catches it. "I'm not a prostitute," I say.

"Anna—"

I don't give him a chance to finish whatever excuse he has prepared. I run from the room and grab Kathleen by the wrist. "I need a drink," I say, slapping her in the face to wake her up and dragging her off the couch.

"I thought you'd never ask," Kathleen says, slurring. We leave our duplex and our new landlord behind. *What an insufferable, rich, handsome man!*

———

Kathleen and I are pounding back Jägerbombs at Eclipse, our favorite watering hole near campus. Eclipse is loud, and the music drowns out my internal monologue so that I don't have to listen to how attractive and desirable Earl Grey is. Kathleen called Jin as we left home, and he met us at the club in his tight-fitting *My Little Pony* shirt, the one that shows off his muscular pecs.

"Have we told you we're moving to Seattle?" I say to Jin.
"*Dios mío,*" he says. "No, this is the first I've heard . . ."
"Well, we're doing it," I say. "In two weeks, after gradua-

tion. Or sooner, since classes are canceled. We just decided to do it on the way here."

Jin shakes his head. "Have fun," he says. I can't tell if he's happy for us or jealous. Probably jealous, because Seattle is totally much cooler than Portland because it has buildings made of glass and steel instead of grass and mud. Plus it's the birthplace of grunge, so Kathleen is excited to finally see a Nirvana show in their hometown.

"Another Jägerbomb?" Jin says, heading to the bar.

"Are you trying to get me wasted?" I say.

"Well, if you're moving away, this might be my last chance to get you smashed and sweep you off your feet," he says. *Oh my, Jin's so funny!*

"Where's Kathleen?" Jin turns around and scans the packed bar. There she is—she's on Jin's back!

"Heeyyyyy," she slurs.

"Okay, you get off him and I'll get us another round of Jägerbombs," I say.

"I'll get him off," Kathleen purrs into Jin's ear. He grins and waves me off.

I stumble toward the bar. How many drinks have I had? Too many, I reckon. I don't usually get drunk, but then again I don't usually have a billionaire CEO showing up in my bedroom with an expensive gift. I don't care how good looking he is—Anna Steal is not someone who can be bought with money. Or bought with things money can buy. When I get to the bar, my inner guidette does a backflip: the bartender is Earl Grey!

"You're drunk, Anna," he says to me, shaking a martini.

"Tell me something I don't know," I say.

"You're exceptionally beautiful," he says.

I blush. "Let me guess: You bought this bar, too?"

He shakes his head. "Oh, Anna," he says, reaching into my soul with his gray eyes and goosing my inner guidette. "For your information, I don't own this bar. I'm a part-time bartender. It's one of my many hobbies. I fell in love with bartending after watching the movie *Cocktail*."

"Never seen it."

"Tom Cruise? *Cocktail?*"

I shake my head. "I don't even know who that is. Sorry."

He laughs his wicked laugh and passes the finished martini to the girl on my left. He takes her money. "You are hilarious, Anna," he says. "Your sense of humor knows no bounds."

"If you really do this part time, why haven't I seen you here before?"

"I normally tend bar at a little club in Seattle, but I'm filling in for a friend here who's sick. Something you have a little experience with." He smirks.

"Whatever," I say. "Give me three Jägerbombs."

"I'm sorry, Anna. I'm taking you home. You're drunk."

"Kathleen or Jin will drive me home," I say.

"They're just as drunk as you are," he says. "I can't take that chance. You're too important to me."

"But you'll let them drive off, drunk?"

"Well, yeah," he says. "I'm not worried about them or about anyone else on the road. The only person I'm worried about in this world is *you*, Anna."

The things he says! He makes me feel like I'm the only girl in the world. I've never felt this special.

"We're leaving now," he says. I hope he's not going to take me on another helicopter ride like earlier in the day, because this time I would, without a doubt, hurl.

"I have to go tell Kathleen and Jin I'm leaving, at least," I say.

Earl leaps over the bar and grips my arm. "Forget them."

"What, are you going to pay them off?"

"When you look at me, you must see a big pile of money," he says. "Is that it?"

When I look at Earl Grey, I don't see a pile of money. I see a pile of SEXY MF. The room begins spinning . . .

Earl throws me over his shoulder and carries me toward the exit.

"Kathleeeeeeen!" I scream.

We stop moving. I look over my shoulder and see why Earl's stopped: Jin. We're in the middle of the dance floor, and dancers begin to clear out around us.

"Put the girl down," Jin says.

"She's drunk, and I'm taking her home," Earl says.

"I can't let you do that."

"Who's going to stop me? *You?* A twenty-one-year-old *brony?*"

Jin nods. "That's right, old man."

Earl lowers me to the ground. I try to tell them to stop fighting over me, that I'm so drunk I'll gladly blow them both in the bathroom. Unfortunately, I can't find my voice. Where did I put it? I don't have time to look for it, because the bro-down of the century is about to begin—over mousy little Anna Steal!

"So how are we going to settle this? Guitar Hero?" Earl says, rolling his sleeves up. The dance floor has cleared off completely and the DJ stops the music.

"Are you serious? What is this, 2008?" Jin says. "You've been watching too much *Gossip Girl.*"

"Maybe so," Earl scoffs. "Then what did you have in mind? We sixty-nine each other on the dance floor and whoever makes the other come first wins?"

Jin shakes his head. "You're real funny—for a rich prick."

"Why don't you call me that to my face?"

"I just did," Jin says.

"Right," Earl says.

"Enough fun and games," Jin says, stepping to within a foot of Earl Grey. "We settle this the only way two men who happen to be in the middle of a dance floor can—"

"With a dance-off," Earl says, interrupting him.

"Actually, I was thinking we could have a fistfight."

"That works too," Earl says. Kathleen stumbles over to me and puts her arm around my shoulders. She's clearly blotto and in no position to intervene either.

Jin balls his hands into fists and stands toe to toe with Earl Grey. Their faces are so close they could kiss. *This could get interesting . . .*

Earl reaches into his pocket and fishes a Benjamin out of his wallet. "One hundred dollars," he says, dangling it in front of Jin's face.

"What's that for?" Jin asks.

"One hundred dollars for you to hit yourself," Earl says.

"You've got to be joking."

Earl opens his wallet again. He stashes the hundred and pulls out a thousand-dollar bill. "One thousand dollars if you will hit yourself for me."

"You think you can buy me? Never," Jin says, slapping the bill out of Earl's hand. The onlookers "oooh" as the bill flutters to the floor.

Earl, unperturbed, reaches back into his wallet and pulls out a bill emblazoned with a portrait of Mitt Romney. "A million dollars," he says, holding it between his face and Jin's. "A million dollars for you to punch yourself . . . in the balls."

Gulp.

Jin lowers his head. There's no way he can turn this down. Fighting over a girl is one thing, but a million dollars is another. He glances at me out of the corner of his eye. "Don't be stupid, Jin," I whisper hoarsely, my voice returning for a split second.

"Fine," Jin mutters.

"What's that? I didn't hear you," Earl says, grinning. Of course he's lying, because everyone at Eclipse heard Jin. It's so quiet you could hear a peen go soft.

"I said, 'Fine.' I'll do it." Jin snaps the million-dollar bill out of Earl's raised hand and stuffs it into his jeans pocket.

"Make it worth my money," Earl says, backing up to give Jin space.

Jin raises his right hand and pulls his fingers in tight. He closes his eyes and whispers a prayer under his breath.

I can't watch him publicly debase himself in such a crude manner. I close my eyes. Kathleen hugs me tight. I can hear the men in the room draw their breath in and hold it. Then, there's a soft thump like a baby bunny in a sack being hit with a mallet . . . and it's over.

The DJ begins playing some music low in the background as the crowd dissipates. I open my eyes. Some students have gathered around a woman who fainted while watching Jin hit himself in the balls. Jin is lying in the fetal position in the middle of the dance floor, his hands cupped around his groin. He's alone. If I weren't so drunk, I would rush over to him and console him. But I would probably throw up on him, and that hardly seems appropriate.

Earl extends a hand to me. "Shall we?"

Kathleen scoops up the dropped thousand-dollar bill and whispers in my ear, "Don't go, Anna," but I shrug her off. Earl has fought for me, and I am his prize at the bottom of his Cracker Jacks tonight.

I feel myself hoisted into the air over Earl's shoulder, and then my vision goes dark . . .

Chapter Seven

EVERYTHING IS QUIET. I slowly open my eyes and feel like I'm being born again, again. The room is large and spacious. I'm fully clothed and in the middle of a fantastically giant bed. The sheets are more comfortable than anything I have ever slept on—the thread count has to be at least two hundred. Maybe even three hundred.

I hear a knock at the door. "Hello?" I say weakly.

The door opens and it's Earl Grey. Instead of his suit and signature smiley-face tie, he is wearing a shiny silver thong and a pair of bright pink Crocs. And nothing else. His hair is slicked back. *Oh my, Mr. Grey . . .*

"Good morning, Anna. How are you doing?"

"Better than last night," I say, finding my voice.

He stands in the doorway and lets me ogle him in his silver willy warmer for a few seconds in silence. I can't believe I made such a fool of myself last night at Eclipse.

"Where am I?" I ask.

"At the most expensive hotel in Portland. The Holiday Inn."

"Oh."

"I just took a dip in the pool," he says. "Hence my lack of clothing. I hope you don't mind."

Don't mind? I love it!

"I thought you were taking me back to my place," I say.

"I was going to, but then your little brony decided to make a scene," he says. "I couldn't risk taking you back to your apartment, only to have Jin and Kathleen show up and start another fight."

"Kathleen's a total B, but she didn't have anything to do with the fight," I say defensively. "And Jin just gets territorial sometimes."

"Jin is dangerous," Earl says. "I tried my best to defuse him."

"I'm sorry things got so out of hand. I've never seen him so . . . bloodthirsty."

"Then all the more reason to stay away from him," Earl says. "You think you know someone, and they go all psycho on you one day . . ."

"So what are your big, dark secrets, Mr. Grey?"

The smirk returns to his face. "I think you know, Anna."

He sidestepped the question the first time we met and he uses expensive body wash, which could only mean . . . "You're gay," I whisper.

"What?"

"I'm sorry, I thought . . ."

"Try again, Anna. Say it. Say what's in your heart. You know my dark secret . . ."

The weird shopping list with the duct tape and rope could only mean . . . "You're a serial killer."

"Try again," he says, rolling his eyes.

Okay. One more time. *You know this, Anna.* He lives a life of luxury insulated by his wealth and privilege, and he has no regard for anyone else's feelings except his own . . . "You're a corporate executive!"

He throws his arms up comically. "While that's true, that's not a secret," he says. "I'm a Dungeon Master, Anna."

What? My inner guidette screeches to a halt on her hamster wheel. I have no clue what he's talking about. "What exactly does a Dungeon Master do?"

"I'm into BDSM," he says.

"Is that a workout thing, like Zumba?"

"No, Anna, it's not anything like Zumba. BDSM is a live-action role-playing game: Bards, Dragons, Sorcery and Magick. I play with women in my dungeon and things can get . . . a little hot."

"Is there no air conditioning in your dungeon?"

Earl sighs. "I mean 'hot' as in sexual. BDSM role playing is very naughty—that's probably why a good girl like you hasn't heard of it."

"Oh, S and M. Like that Rihanna song," I say. "The one about whips and chains."

"The what?"

"Nevermind," I say. Earl is only six years older than me, but sometimes the gulf between our ages seems like something I can't bridge. It's like he's a 104-year-old vampire in a twenty-seven-year-old's body.

"So you're into some kinky shit," I say. "That's your biggest secret?"

"You don't know the depths of my perversion," he says.

I've already seen him at what I figured was the depth of his shame, buying a Nickelback CD. Do I want to know how deep his perversions go? Does he want me to follow him down that rabbit hole, into the dark recesses of his kinky rich-guy mind? I'm just a simple virgin—*oh no.*

"Did we make sandwiches together last night?" I mutter.

"What?"

"It's just my timid way of asking if we did . . . *it.*"

"Are you asking if we had sex last night, Anna?" he says, letting the question hang in the air for a moment. "No."

"Phew. I was worried because I'm . . ." *Uh-oh.* I've said too much. I can't let Earl Grey know I'm a virgin! "My . . . armpits are a little sore. TMI. Sorry."

"I don't think one can ever have too much . . . information," he says suggestively, though I don't know exactly what he's suggesting. He cocks his head to one side and uses his gray eyes to pinch my inner guidette's love handles.

"Anyway, room service will be here shortly with breakfast," he says. "If you want to brush your teeth or take a shower, I'll let you have the restroom first."

"Thanks," I say, getting out of bed. *Woah.* My head starts spinning and it takes a moment to steady myself. Earl watches me, with more bemusement than concern. I stagger to the bathroom and shut the door.

I turn on the water in the shower and wait until it warms up before stripping and stepping in. The water pours over me, washing away my hangover. *I wish Earl were in here with me.* I need Earl Grey. I need his kisses, I need his long fingers, and I need his slicked-back hair . . .

Why didn't he take advantage of me last night? All I'm getting from him are mixed signals. *He buys me tea; he tells me to stay away from him. He practically kidnaps me from a nightclub; he doesn't ravish me in his hotel suite.* I slept next to him all night long, and he didn't touch me. As I rub the cheap and inferior hotel body wash all over my body, I think of Earl Grey touching me . . .

There's a knock at the door. "Breakfast," he says.

"Thanks," I say, my daydream shattered.

~~~

Breakfast is spread out on dozens of trays across the table. Since Earl Grey is, well, Earl Grey, he's ordered two of every item on the room service menu. There's enough food here to feed us for a week. We're both in hotel bathrobes, our naked bodies tantalizingly within arm's reach of one another underneath our robes.

"Why did you buy me the Snooki book?" I say, crunching down on a strawberry-jelly-and-Nutella-smothered slice of toast.

"Because I can," he says, popping a hard-boiled egg into his mouth. "And because I felt bad for leaving you to walk back to Walmart by yourself."

"I'm a big girl," I say, sipping from a glass of hibiscus juice that I've just squeezed. "I can take care of myself."

He chomps into a full head of Napa cabbage. "I'm sure you are. But that doesn't stop me from worrying about you. The world is a bad place. You need to be careful."

I twirl *Spaghetti alla puttanesca* on my fork. "Do I need to be careful around you?"

He looks at me solemnly, his gray eyes full of earnestness. "I already told you: I can be a cruel person," he says, cracking a lobster tail, squirreling a piece of meat out of it, dipping it into fresh melted butter, and sucking it down.

"Then why keep after me?" I run my tongue up and down a stalk of cooked asparagus.

"No matter what I do, no matter how hard I try . . . I can't keep myself away from you," he says, peeling a long carrot and, not to be outdone by the suggestive asparagus show I just put on, fellates the carrot for three solid minutes.

Did you hear that, babe? my inner guidette says. *Earl Grey, the hottest gorilla you've ever laid eyes on, can't stay away from you.* I look down into my egg drop soup, hoping to catch a reflection of what it is that Earl Grey is so taken with, but instead just see a mess of gross-looking bits of shredded egg. I push the bowl away.

"I'd like to drop my eggs in your soup," he says, dipping a strawberry on the end of a long-stemmed fork into a fondue pot of melted chocolate.

I peer up at him, and he's got that wickedly wicked look on his handsomely handsome face again. "Are you hitting on me, Mr. Grey?" I tease, lightly drizzling balsamic vinaigrette on my spinach salad.

He giggles. "I scream, you scream . . . we all scream for ice cream," he says, licking a chocolate-and-vanilla-swirl ice cream cone.

"I'll take that as a yes," I say, carving a turkey and removing the gizzard.

Earl unwraps a McRib, which isn't even on the McDonald menu right now. He smothers the sandwich with barbecue sauce, and asks, "Have you ever worked in fast food?"

I shake my head.

"Too bad," he says, washing down his McRib with a Shamrock Shake, another out-of-season menu item. "I like girls who can take orders."

"Is this your way of asking if I'll play this kinky BDSM game with you, Mr. Grey?"

He sighs, setting down his grilled corn on the cob. "Could you at least act like you're shocked? If you're not shocked by how naughty and perverted my deviant tastes are, it kind of drains all the tension out of our relationship."

"So I should be shocked that you like to do bad stuff to women? Do you sexually abuse them against their will? That would be really shocking."

"No, that's not it at all. I mean, they're into it. I only do it if they like it. Sometimes they're more into it than I am, to be honest."

"But you really injure them? That's why it's shocking?"

"No. They're fine. Some mild redness occurs on their bottoms, but that fades in a few hours."

"I'm not following," I say. "Why am I supposed to be shocked?"

"Anna, if you're game, then why are we tiptoeing around the issue?"

"I don't know," I say. "I've been DTF since we first met."

"Then, without further ado . . ." He sweeps the food off the table, just for dramatic emphasis. He pulls a bugle out of his bathrobe, sounds a long note, and clears his throat. "Let the fucking begin!"

Chapter Eight

AT ONCE, Earl Grey's mouth is upon me. His arms crawl up the back of my robe as his tongue penetrates my lips. Our mouths create an airtight seal, and our tongues battle it out for supremacy. His is the more dominant tongue; I let my tongue go limp and submit fully to Earl Grey. For the first time in my life, I have found my purpose: to be a doormat for this ridiculously wealthy, attractive, impossible-to-resist man.

Suddenly, he withdraws his tongue and releases me from his grasp.

"What's wrong?" I ask.

He narrows his eyes. "Perhaps we shouldn't have started kissing so soon after eating. Your mouth tastes like you ate an entire garlic bulb."

"That's because I did," I say.

He sighs. "Go brush your teeth. I'll wait here."

I lower my gaze and walk to the bathroom. I close the door. There's only one toothbrush on the sink, and it belongs to Earl Grey. I pick it up and run the bristles over my lips. It's like a six-inch piece of Earl. I slide the toothbrush into my mouth and, angling my head and neck, slowly ease it down my throat. *Mmmmm . . .* I can't wait to deep throat Earl's—

"Hurry up, woman," he says from the next room, startling me. I drop the toothbrush straight down my throat. I'm such an idiot! My inner guidette rolls her eyes. The toothbrush is caught in my esophagus; I can't breathe. I clutch my throat and try coughing, but it's no use. My body crumples to the floor . . .

"What is going on in there, Anna?" Earl says with concern in his voice.

I try to call out, but nothing comes out of my mouth except drool.

The door swings open, and Earl Grey stands above me. Earl Grey, my savior!

"My God, Anna, what are you doing on the floor?"

I motion to my throat with both hands. Earl, immediately sensing the gravitas of the situation, props me into a sitting position. He kneels behind me and wraps his arms around me. He attempts the Heimlich maneuver, but it's no use. I'm fading into unconsciousness quickly . . .

Earl lays me on my back and tilts my head back. "I can't lose you, Anna," he says. "I can't!"

He pushes his long fingers into my mouth. I feel them creeping down my throat. He carefully backs his fingers out, holding the toothbrush between his impossibly long index and middle fingers. I breathe again, and it's the sweetest breath I've ever taken. Air is like cable TV: you don't appreciate it until you don't have it.

"Thank you," I say to Earl. If his fingers weren't so freak-ishly long, I would be dead right now.

"I don't know what I would do without you, Anna," he says. It's an emotional moment, and we both pause to gaze at each other. *Is he going to kiss me again?*

Earl stands up and helps me to my feet, for the second time in two days. Or the third time. I'm losing track of how often he saves me from myself.

"Now brush your teeth," he says. "That garlic is really quite overpowering."

I nod. He closes the door on his way out of the bath-room. *No playing around now. Just brush your teeth, go out there, and ride his D to O-Town,* my inner guidette says. *You got this, babe!*

I squeeze out a dollop of mint toothpaste onto Earl Grey's toothbrush and begin polishing my teeth. *The faster you do this, the sooner you can lose your virginity to Earl Grey. Mmmmm . . . Earl Grey . . .* The more I think about him, the more the toothbrush becomes him, and I swear I don't know how it happens but thirty seconds later I'm on the floor, choking again.

~~~~~~

I'm lying on my back on the bed, the same position I started the morning in. The big difference is that Earl Grey is now hovering over me. Well, not literally hovering, because that would mean we're in zero gravity or that Earl can levitate, but you get the idea. He's, like, on top of me. We're both in our robes still. He has just saved me from choking twice in the span of three minutes. My breath still reeks of garlic.

"I've been waiting for this moment forever," he says.

"We just met last week," I say. "How can that be?"

"You take everything so literally, Anna. I love that about you."

"So you haven't been waiting for this moment forever?"

He laughs that wicked Earl Grey laugh. "Oh, Anna . . ."

Earl unties the cloth belt holding my robe together. I shudder. *Oh my . . .* We're really going to do this. He slowly opens my robe, exposing my pale skin to the air. He runs the back of his fingers down the length of my body from my neck to my untrimmed thigh hair. He smiles at me, though he smiles most of the time. Maybe I should just start mentioning when he's not smiling? That would be easier.

"I've never done this before," I say meekly. I shut my eyes in embarrassment.

"Never had sex in a hotel room?" he says, cradling my face in his hand. I kiss his palm.

"Never had sex . . . at all," I say.

He doesn't say anything. I open my eyes.

"I know, Anna," he says. "I've read transcripts of all your therapist appointments from the time you were sixteen until last week. You don't think you're desirable, but you don't know the power you have . . ."

"You're not mad?" I say.

"Why would I be?"

I shrug. "I didn't think most guys wanted to date virgins. We're not very experienced, and we usually have emotional hang-ups involving sex."

"Who said we're dating?"

Gulp. It's like I was following the bread crumbs on a trail to his heart, but a big bird came along and ate them all. The trail of bread crumbs has gone cold.

"I already told you, I'm not a 'girlfriend' kind of guy, Anna," he says, scolding me. "But that reminds me . . ."

Earl reaches a hand into his robe and pulls out a thick manila envelope. He sits up on his knees and hands it to me. *Uh-oh. What is this?*

"It's a quiz," he says.

"A quiz?" I say, holding it. "What kind of quiz?"

"The kind you might find in *Cosmo*," he says, and the smirk is back. How I missed his smirk! "It's a sex quiz, baby."

Chapter Nine

MY ROBE IS TIED AGAIN, and it doesn't look like Earl Grey and I are going to be jumping back into bed anytime soon. He's relaxing on the bed, watching oiled-up men in their underwear roll around with each other on some WWE wrestling program. He's giving me a chance to read over the entire quiz, and refuses to even go to first base with me until I've filled it out. This isn't how I expected to spend my Sunday; in some ways, it's even more tedious than studying for my final exams.

Name: _____

My ideal man is:
   a. Smart
   b. Funny
   c. Good looking
   d. Wealthy
   e. Sociopathic
   f. All of the above

I feel sexiest when I'm wearing:
   a. New shoes
   b. A slinky black dress

   c. Nipple clamps

   d. All of the above

I'm afraid of:

   a. Being flogged

   b. Being tied up

   c. Running out of toilet paper in a public restroom

   d. None of the above

My favorite body part is:

   a. My butt

   b. My boobs

   c. My eyes

   d. My partner's eyes

Toys I would like to try include:

   a. Vibrators

   b. Butt plugs

   c. *Hello Kitty*–brand toasters

   d. All of the above

I am:

   a. Team Edward

   b. Team Jacob

   c. Team Edward Does Jacob

I find it really hot when a man:

   a. Listens to me

   b. Cooks dinner for me

   c. Canes my ass like a Singapore prison warden

One extracurricular activity I've always wanted to try is:
a. "Dirty Sanchez"
b. "Rusty trombone"
c. "Amish plow"
d. "Abraham Lincoln"

In a relationship, I prefer to be:
a. Submissive
b. Dominant
c. Awake

One day, I'd really like to:
a. Meet Tom Cruise
b. Go skydiving
c. Have sex with Earl Grey
d. All of the above, at the same time

The amount of pain I can tolerate on a scale of 1 to 5, where 1 is "none" and 5 is "listening to anything by Fergie or the Black-Eyed Peas," is:
1–2–3–4–5

And there's more.

⤜⤏

I look up from the quiz at Earl in disbelief. "You actually want me to fill this out?"

He turns the television volume down. "That was kind of the idea, Anna," he says.

Every time he says my name, a chill runs down my spine. That doesn't change the fact that I'm irritated with him. He won't be using his charm and good looks on me, not this time.

"You're out of your damn mind," I say. "I'm not filling anything out."

"If you don't, then . . ."

"Then what? You won't make love to me?"

He cackles, then growls, then cackles. "I don't make love, Anna. I hardly play. I mean, I play hard."

Woah. Just hearing him say the word "hard" makes me want to fill out the sex quiz. But no! I have to stand my ground. *Be strong, Anna,* my inner guidette says. *Don't let this juicehead push you around.*

"What happened to you as a child to make you this way?" I ask Earl.

"What way?" he says defensively.

"So afraid of forming any real emotional connection."

"I resent that remark," he says. "I'm a people person."

I shake my head. "You use people, Earl. The billion people who work for you are nothing more than grains of sand that make up a beach that you relax on, with a piña colada in one hand and a blond receptionist in the other."

"You don't know what you're talking about," he says. "I've never had a piña colada in my life."

"I may not be the smartest person in this room, but I'm not some stupid college kid," I say, emboldened by the rise

I'm getting out of him. Actually, I am a stupid college kid; hopefully, he doesn't pick up on my verbal slip.

"Stop this at once, before you say something you regret," he says.

"You're not a people person, Mr. Grey. You dispose of employees with the slightest provocation. You buy and sell companies based on whom you're dating, without regard to the employees whose lives you affect when you act so willy-nilly. You can't even enter into a relationship without your partner answering a twelve-hundred-page *Cosmo* quiz. You're afraid of people."

Earl Grey, no longer smirking, shakes his head and lowers his gaze. Have I broken through the great Earl Grey's ego?

"The quiz is only a thousand one hundred eighty-seven pages, but . . . you're right. You're right, Anna," he says.

"I am?"

"Yes," he says. "Fine. Don't answer the quiz questions. We can discuss it later."

Did he just cede a point to me? I think he did! Score one for the away team.

"Now, if you're not man enough to slay dragons with me without some stupid quiz, I'm leaving," I say.

His eyes open wide. Now I've shocked the dark and dangerous Earl Grey!

"Don't go," he says, a hint of desperation in his voice. "There's something I need to show you first. Get dressed."

Chapter Ten

WITH MY BACK TURNED to Earl, I slip my underwear on and adjust my bra underneath my robe. Out of the corner of my eye, I catch a glimpse of Earl changing. I've already seen every part of his body except for his dangling participle. He wouldn't make me get dressed just to see that, would he? He must have something else planned for us.

"Are we going somewhere?" I ask.

"My apartment in Seattle," he says, zipping his jeans. Each new outfit he wears is a revelation. His skinny jeans ride low on his scrumptious hips.

I pick up the quiz and we head for the elevators. I didn't know we had elevators in Portland! Earl presses the button for the roof.

"Oh," I say. "I don't know if I'm up for a three-hour helicopter ride today . . ."

"We're not taking my helicopter," he says.

When we step out of the elevator and onto the rooftop, I see what Earl means. "A private jet!" I scream.

He smiles. "The helicopter is okay, but when I need to jet somewhere fast . . . well, I use a jet. Hop in, baby."

He presses a button on his keychain remote and raises the jet's glass cockpit. I climb a short ladder and settle into the rear seat. Earl takes the front seat where the controls are.

"You know what kind of jet this is?" he says, pressing a button to lower the glass shield. I have no idea, and he doesn't give me a chance to answer anyway. "It's an F-14 Tomcat. The same fighter jet that Tom Cruise flew in *Top Gun*."

"Is he some kind of pilot? I thought you said he was a bartender?"

Earl fires up the engine. "No, baby, he's an actor. Tom Cruise played Maverick in the 1986 film *Top Gun*. Man, I can't believe you haven't seen it. That just blows my mind."

I shake my head. "Before my time, I guess."

Earl ignores me and backs the jet up to give us the maximum amount of runway space on the Holiday Inn rooftop. "There were only seven hundred twelve of these bad boys built," he says. "Most of them were scrapped by the US Navy; a few were sold to foreign governments. This is the only one in private use in the world. Put this on." He hands me a helmet with GOOSE printed on it.

"Who's Goose?"

"You are, today," he says, strapping on his own helmet that reads MAVERICK.

"You really like this Tom Cruise guy," I observe.

The jet has come to a halt on the rooftop. He turns and frowns at me. "What are you implying?"

"Nothing, geez."

"Anyway," he continues, "You're in for a treat. We should be in Seattle in no time. This jet can go up to fifteen hundred miles per hour."

Holy speed of sound! "We're going to die," I whisper.

"Not on my watch you won't," Earl says. "How many times have I saved your life so far?"

"Three. Or four," I say meekly.

"Exactly. Buckle up. We're about to take a ride into the Danger Zone." He pauses. "Sorry, poor choice of words. It's from a song on the *Top Gun* soundtrack."

Earl pops a cassette out of the F-14's tape deck and searches in the glove compartment for a different album. "No *Danger Zone* today. I think this song is more appropriate," he says, popping in a new tape. Most people my age probably don't know what "cassette tapes" are, but I know all about them thanks to Kathleen. When I get home, I'll ask her about this *Top Gun* movie. She might have it on VHS or laserdisc.

The music that Earl has picked out starts off with lyrics comparing a woman to cherry pie. Earl hums along, flipping various controls and doohickeys. I don't want to make him feel any more uncomfortable about our six-year age difference, so I keep my mouth shut and don't ask who the band is. They sound embarrassingly bad, like Adam Lambert if he were straight. I don't always pick up on double meanings, but even I can tell the song is about sex. "Mixing up the batter while she licks the beater"? I mean, c'mon, guys. That's just crude.

"And one more thing," Earl says, turning around. "Take your finger out of your nose."

"Sorry," I say, pulling it out. I've got to stop being such a disgusting idiot around him!

I feel the jet inch forward. The engine roars, drowning out the awful music. We speed up and before I know it we're airborne! I look out the window and see the Holiday Inn below us getting smaller and smaller by the second. Soon, the entire quaint city of Portland shrinks from view. What was life like before I met Earl Grey and started going on these crazy adventures? I can hardly remember. It's like I was born yesterday. That's something Dad's always telling me: "What were you, born yesterday?" I never understood his question, because of course he knows my birthday. Now I think I get what he was saying. It's an amazing feeling.

"Watch this," Earl says over the noise of the jet's engine. He angles the plane directly toward a snow-capped mountain.

"Are you trying to kill us?" I scream.

"Hush, baby," he says. "That's Mount Rainier, one of the most dangerous active volcanoes in the world. But don't worry—it hasn't erupted in over a hundred and fifty years."

"I'm not worried about it erupting," I mutter, bracing myself for our imminent collision with the mountain.

When we're less than a hundred yards away from impact, Earl presses a button and three missiles shoot out from each wing and explode into the side of Mount Rainier, making a hole large enough for us to fly through to the other side!

When we're in the clear, I tell Earl just how amazing that was.

"I do this kind of stuff all the time," he says. "I can guarantee you'll never be bored around Earl Grey."

No way, not in a million years, I think. Well, maybe in a million years, because who knows what the ramifications of extending one's lifespan to such a length are? I can see, yeah, in a million years maybe two people would get bored of each other. But in fifty or sixty years or whatever? No way.

I look back and see that the hole Earl shot in Mount Rainier is in the shape of a heart. *Swoon!* As the long-dormant volcano erupts plumes of thick, black smoke behind us into the air, all I can think about is this: I'm in love.

Chapter Eleven

WE'RE AT EARL GREY'S penthouse apartment at the top of one of the tallest, most elegant-looking steel erections in downtown Seattle. It's directly across the street from his office; he commutes back and forth using a zipline stretched between the two buildings. The inside of Earl Grey's bachelor pad is amazing. It's almost all black and white, with a few splashes of puce and cadmium red. It's just perfect.

"This is beautiful, Mr. Grey," I say. "I wish I had an interior decorator to do my place up like this."

"I did it myself," he says.

"Oh."

"No homo," he says forcefully.

I shake my head. "I wasn't thinking that. Was that what you were thinking I was thinking? Because that's definitely not what I was thinking."

(It's totally what I was thinking.)

"What do I have to do to prove to you how not-gay I am?" he asks.

You could just shut up and press "start" on the sex machine. I don't say that, though, because I think he likes the cat-and-mouse game. Every time I'm too direct with him he gets all emo and shuts down. Instead, I say, "What did you bring me all the way here for?"

"To show you this," he says, leading me into a reading room. His library is huge and filled with thousands of books. I wonder what else of his is huge. Probably his kitchen.

Earl runs his long fingers over the books at eye level on one of his many bookcases. His fingers stop on one book. *Twilight*.

"You brought me all the way to your bachelor pad to show me *Twilight*? I've got news for you, I've read it like a hundred times," I say, rolling my eyes.

Earl smirks. He gently tilts the book out by its spine and the bookcase next to us begins to swing into the wall!

The walls of the room on the other side of the open bookcase are painted entirely black. "Is this your dungeon?" I ask him.

"You're impressively perceptive, Anna," Earl says, nodding. "I call it my 'Room of Doom.'"

"And you want me to go in there. With you."

He nods, waving a hand toward the secret passage. "Ladies first."

The first thing I notice is the smell: Nag Champa incense and dirty laundry. The room is illuminated only by black light, but I can see enough to tell this is the kind of closet R. Kelly wouldn't mind being trapped in. The room is tiny compared to the rest of Earl Grey's apartment. There's barely enough room for the waterbed. Whips, chains, ropes, riding crops, paddles, and iron shackles are hung up on the walls next to black-light posters—really trippy black-light posters. "Room of Doom"? More like the "Dorm Room of Doom."

I feel Earl's hand on my left shoulder. He's breathing into my ear. "Welcome to my world, baby."

"Do you bring all your dates here?"

"I don't know if I'd call them 'dates,'" he says. "They are, more accurately, LARPers. 'LARP' stands for 'live-action role playing.'"

"I saw that term used in the quiz."

"The quiz you so stubbornly refuse to fill out," he says, trying to act all exasperated. I think he's putting on more of a show now.

"These LARPers . . . If they're not dates, then what are they? Volunteers? Where do you meet them?"

Earl picks up a leather toy that looks sort of like a whip, only with multiple leather strips hanging off the end. "There are women who LARP professionally," he says. "They're all over Craigslist."

I laugh at the thought of him trolling for women on Craigslist. Surely someone as good looking and rich as Earl Grey doesn't need to resort to picking up girls on the Internet! "You're kidding," I say.

He shakes his head. "I know, it just seems so dirty to meet women on Craigslist."

"Dirty and gross," I say.

"It's just one of my fifty shames, Anna," he says, lowering his head.

"And you use these . . . *things* on them? You torture them?" I ask, motioning to his sex toys.

"If the game calls for it. Take this flogger, for instance," he says, perking up and swinging the leather tool through the air. "I'll use this on a woman's back, and ass, and legs."

"And these LARPers like it when you beat them?"

"Oh yes," he says. "Pleasure and pain are two sides of the same coin. At another level, though, my LARPers want to please me. I am the Dungeon Master, after all."

Control freak. But damn! What a sexy control freak.

"So you want me to role-play with you?"

"Eventually," he says, grinning.

"So how does this erotic role playing work?"

"I make the rules, and you obey them. It's very simple. Follow the rules, and you will be rewarded. Break the rules, and you will be punished," he says. "It's about exploring each other's limits within a codified system of punishments and rewards. It's about trust."

"What do I get out of the whole deal? I don't know if pretending I'm an elf being whipped is really my thing."

"I see you as more of a faery than as an elf, but we can get into specifics later. What I get out of our arrangement is you, submitting to my every whim," he says. "And what you get is Earl Grey."

Wow. Somebody thinks highly of themselves.

"We don't have to start out role-playing today; we can

ease our way into our characters with time. I need you right now, though—any way I can get you."

Oh my. Earl reaches a hand out to me. I take it in mine, and he leads me to the waterbed. I am no longer hung over, but I'm so nervous that I'm shaking.

"Let's get comfortable, shall we?" he says, removing his calculator watch and setting it on top of the nightstand by the bed.

I take a cue from him and remove my yellow LiveStrong bracelet, setting it next to his watch.

"Let's get even more comfortable, hmmmm?" he says, removing his pink Crocs.

I remove my tennis shoes and nearly choke on the smell of my own dirty socks. They've been through a lot in the past two days. If Earl can smell them, he doesn't give any indication. I just hope he's not a foot fetishist.

"That's not quite comfortable enough, though," he says, grinning. I still cannot believe that this attractive, kinky man is interested in me.

"Oh, it's not, is it?" I say playfully, putting my arms up the back of my shirt, unhooking my bra, and twisting out of it like it's a straitjacket. I dangle my red push-up bra off the end of a finger and toss it at Earl.

He catches it. "Oh my, Anna," he says. He drops my bra to the floor, and reaches his own hands up underneath his black T-shirt. Thirty seconds of fumbling around later, Earl pulls a lacy black bra out from under his shirt. "Two can play at this game," he says with a wicked flash of wickedness.

"Were you wearing that since we left the hotel?" I ask.

"I told you I'm kinky, baby," he says. There's an awkward pause. "Let's just get naked. Ready, set . . . go!"

We strip the rest of our clothes off at record speed. Soon, we're both as naked as the day we were born. Except, y'know, we're not covered in blood and attached to our mothers by umbilical cords.

I run my eyes up and down Earl Grey's breathtaking body, and my eyes stop to rest on his magnificent length. I want to grab it, swing it around, and bite into it—but, somehow, I'm able to contain myself. It's probably for the best, because I don't think Earl wants bite marks on his little milkman.

I'm not the only one checking someone out—Earl is taking in every inch of my body with his gray eyes. I feel naked before him, mostly because I don't have any clothes on.

"You're beautiful, Anna," he says.

I'm not good at taking compliments, but I try my best. "You're more beautiful," I say.

"I know," he says. "You ready to do this?"

"Absolutely."

Earl Grey takes my hand and guides me onto the waterbed . . .

Chapter Twelve

"**W**ow, that was amazing," I say, sprawled out on my back in Earl Grey's bed.

"Thank you," he says. "I've never had three orgasms in a row before just holding someone's hand and sitting down on a bed. I can't imagine what the actual sex is going to be like."

"You don't have to imagine," I say.

"You're right," he says. He's hovering over me again, but this time we're both naked. I can feel his stick shift delectably pressing into my stomach. Kathleen would call him a "Trent Reznor," since he has a nine-inch nail. (Don't worry—I don't get her references either.)

My nipples are hard, either from my heightened state of arousal or because it's a little chilly in the Dorm Room of Doom.

"I want you so bad," Earl says, "but I'm going to make you wait."

"Haven't we waited long enough?" I say.

"I'm going to kiss every part of your body," he says. "Starting with your feet and working my way up . . ."

Quintuple crap.

"How about if you start a little higher, like at my knees maybe?" I say.

"Anna, there's no need to be shy," he says, backing himself down the bed toward the lower part of my body. He kneels at the foot of the bed and bends over my feet. "I love your scent, Anna," he says, placing his nose an inch away from my toes and inhaling deeply. His eyes grow wide with surprise. "But, perhaps, I shall start with your knees. Good idea."

He kisses my kneecaps, which is a little weird, because there aren't many nerve endings there. Or the skin is too callused. I don't know—like I ever look at my knees? When he moves his lips to the back of my knees, raising my legs slightly to accommodate his mouth, I let out a yelp. It tickles. Maybe kissing every single part of my body isn't the way to get me ready for his meatsicle.

He moves on to kissing my quads, and before long I feel his lips on the insides of my thighs . . . Now we're getting somewhere. When his mouth is a half-inch away from my lady parts, though, Earl Grey skips up to my belly. "Are you teasing me?" I say.

"Whatever do you mean, Miss Steal?" he says, flashing me that toothy grin and winking.

He continues his exploration of my body, finally reaching my bust. He flicks his tongue at one of my aching nipples to wet it, and then blows on it. Just when I think he's done toying with it, he clamps his mouth down and begins sucking greedily. My nipples are now so hard they could cut diamonds. Earl looks up at me and smiles.

"Your lip!" I say. "It's bleeding."

He pats his lip and looks at his hand. *Oh no* . . . He cut his lip on my hardened point!

"I guess I won't be going down on you today," he says, sighing.

"Do you have AIDS or something?" I say.

"Not anymore," he says.

"I give blood every three months," I say. "I've never had sex. I'm pretty sure I'm clean."

"I want to taste you, Anna, and I will. Another day, preferably after my lip is healed."

"Okay," I whisper.

Earl places one of his long fingers on my lips and I instinctively begin sucking it. He withdraws his finger and I watch him slowly approach my sex, hidden deep within my untamed thatch of pubic hair. His hand disappears into my pubes, and he searches for my love button.

Ah! Oh. He's found it. This feels . . . good.

"Do you like that, Anna?" he says, running his finger over my most sensitive spot like it's a MacBook trackpad.

"Yes, Mr. Grey," I say.

"Is this how you pleasure yourself?"

I don't. The blank look on my face says it all.

"You have climaxed before, haven't you, Anna?"

I shake my head. "Never."

"You've never even touched yourself?"

Again, I shake my head.

Earl sighs. "You've been missing out. If I had your gorgeous body, I would spend every day lying in bed, discovering myself. I would never leave the house."

"That doesn't sound healthy," I say. I focus my attention on what Earl's doing with his hand . . .

"You're so wet," he says, dipping a finger inside me.

Duh. *I've been going through three pairs of panties a day since I met you, Earl Grey.*

"Moan," I moan. "Moan, moan, moooooooan."

Just as I'm reaching the peak of my arousal, he withdraws his finger. "I'm going to assume you are not taking birth control pills," Earl says.

I never expected to have sex, ever, so that's a big "no." I shake my head.

"It's okay," he says. He leans over to the nightstand and pulls a string of condom packets out. The packets are connected to form one long foil snake, which disappears over the edge of the bed. There have to be at least thirty condoms on it. *How many condoms is he going to wear?*

Earl tears one of the packets open and slides the condom onto his turgid python. "I'm surprised that fit," I mutter. *Did I say that out loud? What is this man doing to me?*

He just laughs. "These condoms are tailored," he says.

"So you went into a store somewhere and they measured you? And what—made them just for you?"

"The perks of being part of the .00001%, Anna," he says.

Wow. Um, wow.

Earl Grey rises above me, towering over my naked, quivering woman-flesh. I can't believe this is happening—it's too much like a wet dream about Robert Pattinson to be real.

"Are you ready for my love gun?" he says.

Uh-oh. "What's a love gun? Is that a sex toy?"

"No," he says. "I'm talking about my penis."

"Oh," I say. "Then yes. Fire away."

He positions himself between my legs. I pull my legs up, bent at the knees to expose my sex to him. He has a mischievous look on his face as he kneels and scoots toward me. He places the sheathed tip of his erection at the entrance to my garden of delights like a dart player lining up a shot. I close my eyes and prepare for the sexy time to begin . . .

. . . and Earl is gone. I hear him slip back off the bed and run off. *What the hell?*

I open my eyes and spot him. He's in the library, about thirty yards away. He's in a low crouch. Without warning, Earl begins jogging straight at me, picking up speed the closer he gets to the waterbed. By the time he reaches the entrance to the Dorm Room of Doom, he's running at full speed. I close my eyes again and spread my legs wide to receive him. He slams his pink torpedo into me, followed by the rest of his body on top of me. My skull crashes into the headboard.

"Ow!" I yell.

He's breathing heavy, and stops to catch his breath. "Was that an 'ow' for your head, or for your panini?"

"Both, I think," I say, wincing.

"I told you I play hard," he says.

I open my mouth to say something, anything, but I have no witty comeback for him. I think I have a concussion. He kisses me on the forehead. "You're tight," he says.

"I'm a virgin," I say, before correcting myself: "I was a virgin."

"Actually, you're still a virgin," Earl says, looking down at his point of entry. "I'm in the wrong hole."

He pulls himself out and changes into a fresh condom. "Let's try this again," he says. I must have a look on my face like some poor girl on a blind date with Chris Brown, because he adds, "No acrobatics this time. We'll take it easy."

He kneels between my legs again and slides easily into me. This time, I'm sure he has the right hole because it doesn't feel like I have to take a dump. "Now I'm going to move around," he says, swiveling his hips slowly. *Is he going to announce every action in bed?*

It hurts, but yet it feels . . . good. The physical connection between our bodies strengthens the emotional connection we already have. "You want more?" he says.

"Yes," I whimper, and he thrusts forward. He swings his hips to the side, then up, then down, like he's trying to sign his name on the back wall of my carnal cave. Time slows down as Earl speeds up; I'm somewhere in a blissful land where nothing in my life matters anymore, where Earl Grey's money and power are distant concerns. Right now, in this moment, we are just two people doing the eternal dance between man and woman. I quiver, and shake, and try to contain the pleasure coursing through my body. It's no use—he's driving me over the edge, into a world of ecstasy I didn't know could exist. The only other time I've felt this good was when I shot smack with Kathleen.

"I want you to climax," Earl says. No, he doesn't just "say"—he *commands* me to climax. For him, I will. For him, I'll do anything. The walls of my pink palace, responding to his voice, spasm around him. As waves of pleasure roll over my body, he screams my name and I feel his Mount Rainier erupt inside me.

He withdraws and falls onto his back on the waterbed. We both take a moment to catch our breath. After a few minutes, he turns to face me. "Are you hurt?" he asks.

I close my eyes. Hurt? *Yes. No. I don't know.* It's such a complicated question. Physically, my nether regions feel like they've been through World War III. I definitely don't want to look at the white bed sheets with the lights on. But once I get past the physical pain of losing my virginity, all I can think about is how the act of joining our two bodies brought me closer to another person than I'd ever thought possible. And not just *any* other person, but Earl Grey. It's like our mutual orgasm was a sign from the heavens that we were destined for each other, like our bodies are in sync at both a biological and cosmic level.

"I actually feel kind of great," I say.

Earl doesn't say anything.

"Earl?" I say, opening my eyes and looking at him. I guess there won't be any Round Two this afternoon, because Earl Grey is sound asleep. I place my head on his chest, and soon I'm drifting off as well . . .

Chapter Thirteen

WHEN I WAKE UP from my nap, I'm alone in bed—*Earl Grey's* bed. He's left a green lava lamp lit on the nightstand, and it looks totally sweet bathed in the Dorm Room of Doom's black light. If you would have told me a week ago that I'd be here, I'd have called you crazy. Insane. Wacko. But it's real. Well, at least as real as sparkly vampires.

In the distance, I hear mournful tambourine playing. I get out of bed to investigate. I pull on my panties and find Earl's button-down shirt, which smells faintly like his coconut-lime body wash. I slip into his shirt and follow the sound of the music into the living room.

While I slept, the sun set and downtown Seattle lit up, marking the end of another gorgeous day in the Emerald City. The view through the floor-to-ceiling windows of the city at night is amazing, but not as amazing as the view of Earl Grey. He's still naked, and he's sitting on a barstool with a tambourine in his left hand. He shakes it rhythmically to a tune only he can hear in his head. His eyes are closed, and he's completely lost in his playing. He has a sad, anguished expression on his face, like white guitar players have when they're playing the blues. A single lamp beside him illuminates his body like he's on display in a museum. *I'd pay twenty dollars for the Earl Grey exhibit.*

I walk quietly toward him, drawn in by his forlorn tambourine playing. He's holding the instrument with the same long fingers that were all over me. I smile inwardly at the memory, even though it happened only a few hours ago. I can't wait for those long fingers to be on me again.

He must hear me approaching, because he stops playing and opens his eyes. "Hello, Anna," he says.

"You can keep playing," I say. I hope he's not mad at me for disturbing him.

"Playing the tambourine . . . or playing you?"

Oh my.

"You're good," I say. "At both, ah, 'instruments.' What was that song?"

"A little something by Poison that I have vague memories of my mother singing to me when I was a child. The song is called 'Every Rose Has Its Thorn.'"

"Which one of us is the rose?"

"Ask me later," he says. He looks me up and down, sipping my body in like a baby drinking apple juice from a sippy cup. "*Risky Business.* I like it."

"Risky what?"

"The dress shirt and underwear look. Nevermind," he says.

He seems sadder now than when he was playing, so I change the topic of conversation. "How long have you been playing tambourine?"

"Since junior high school," he says. "The tambourine is

only one of many percussion instruments I'm trained on."
I try to imagine the broad-shouldered, sexy beast before me
as a child, but it's impossible.

"Anna, your finger is in your nose again," he says.

I yank it out. "Sorry."

"Don't apologize. You have no idea how badly it turns
me on when you do that," he says. "If you pick your nose in
public, I might not be able to stop myself from taking you
where you stand."

"Yikes."

"Which reminds me: Are you feeling okay? From earlier,
I mean," he says, his eyes wandering to my nether regions.

"Yes," I say. "More than okay."

"Good. I'm glad," he says. "Are you hungry?"

I shrug. "I had a big breakfast. Remember?"

"How could I forget? Then what *are* you hungry for, if
not food?"

"I think you know the answer to that, Mr. Grey."

He hops off his barstool and we head back into the Dorm
Room of Doom. Looks like Round Two will happen after
all . . .

Back in his waterbed, Earl flips me over onto my stomach.
"On your hands and knees," he growls.

"Yes," I say, raising myself.

I feel a firm hand slap my behind. "When we're in the
Room of Doom, address me properly, Anna. 'Yes, *Sir*.'"

"Yes, Sir," I say. It feels so natural.

"Good girl," he says, rubbing the spot on my bottom where he spanked me. I love his touch.

I hear him tearing into a foil condom packet. "I'm going to do it to you doggy style," he says.

"Should I bark?" I ask.

"Why would you bark?"

"Well, I thought maybe that's why it's called 'doggy style' . . ."

"I'd prefer if you didn't bark like a dog," he says. "I'm not into bestiality."

"Well, someone's not very kinky," I mutter.

"Just hold still," he says, thrusting powerfully into me from behind. He grabs ahold of my hair and pulls gently. "You like?" he asks.

"Yes, Sir," I say as he slides in and out of me. It's not as romantic as earlier, but there's a raw, primal feeling to what we're doing that makes me want to howl like a wolf. I'm afraid if I do, though, he'll stop, and I can't bear the thought of him stopping midcoitus.

I moan, and then moan again, and again, and again, until his rhythmic thrusting pushes me over the edge. This time, my orgasm turns my arms and legs to jelly, and I collapse on the bed.

"Turn around and sit up," he orders me.

"Yes, Sir," I say, giggling. He's screwed me silly! I can barely move, but I somehow manage to sit up. I rest my back against the headboard.

"Now I'm going to make babies with your face, Anna," he says, crawling toward me on his knees. *Can that thing fit in my mouth?* I wonder, staring at him. I have a horrible flashback to earlier in the day, when I choked on his toothbrush— twice. This is no toothbrush.

Earl straddles my body and points his man of steel at my mouth. Up this close, Grey's anatomy looks like a nineteen-inch nail.

"Don't be afraid," he says. "You can do it. It's just like sword swallowing."

Gulp. "I've never swallowed a sword before," I say, staring down the barrel of his love gun.

"Oh," he says. "That's weird. Well, I'll give you a lesson then."

"In sword swallowing?"

"Yes," he says. "In sword swallowing. Get dressed."

Back in the living room, Earl teaches me the ancient art of sword swallowing. The trick, he says, is to suppress the muscles and processes involved in swallowing; one does not literally "swallow" the sword. Much to my chagrin, he teaches me using a samurai sword, and not his gravy-maker. I'm not very good at first, but after a couple of hours I can take the sharpened blade down my throat to the hilt. It's late, and Earl has an important business meeting in the morning, so we go to sleep without having sex again. Pacing ourselves isn't such a bad idea, especially since we still have more than half the book left.

Chapter Fourteen

I WAKE TO THE SOUND of my cell phone buzzing on the nightstand. I fumble around for it with my eyes half closed, and by the time I have it in my hand it stops. Twelve missed calls and several text messages, all from Kathleen. I scan through them quickly.

where r u
dammit anna answer ur phone
*jin ruptured one of his testicles and i had to take him to the dr.
 i hope ur happy*
tell ur new boyfriend hi

Sigh. I want to text her back and let her know I'm okay, that Earl Grey isn't my boyfriend (because he "doesn't do the girlfriend thing"), and that I'm saying a prayer for Jin's testicles. I can't text her though, not now—all she'll do is bring me down, and the last thing I need is reality intruding upon my graphic sexual fantasy.

It's ten in the morning, and Earl Grey is long gone from the bed. He hasn't completely abandoned me, because I'm still wearing Earl's shirt from last night; it's like I've skinned him and am wearing his flesh. Only it's less creepy by like a million times. I swing my legs out of the bed and stand up. Sunlight is streaming into the apartment. I make my way to the kitchen, and find a note folded on top of an iPad. I open the note.

Anna—

Top of the morning to you!

When you're ready for breakfast, just tell my butler and he'll cook something for you. His name is Data. He is well trained in the culinary arts, so please take advantage of him.

The iPad is yours. We need a way to keep in touch while I'm at work, and I hate texting. It makes me feel like a thirteen-year-old girl. So, since you told me you've never had a computer or even an e-mail address, I thought you would enjoy the tablet (although I must confess I don't understand how you made it through four years of college without the Internet). Just turn it on (press the button!) and touch the "Mail" app. I've set you up with your own Hotmail account.

I'll be home from work later this evening; you're welcome to stay at the apartment all day and watch movies, play board games, etc. I can fly you back to Portland this evening.

E. G.

P.S. You are amazing in bed. I quite enjoyed sticking my thingie inside your thingie. ;)

Oh my. My very own iPad. And if that wasn't enough, he's given me my very own Hotmail account! Not only did I lose my virginity within the past twenty-four hours, I also now have e-mail. I want to turn the iPad on and give it a test drive, but my hunger is more immediate.

"Looking for me, Miss Steal?" a man behind me says in a monotone voice. I whip around and am face-to-face with a pale man wearing a green-and-black spandex jumpsuit. I try to back away from this strange person, but am trapped between him and the kitchen counter. If I can reach the iPad in time, I can e-mail Earl Grey and have him call the police . . .

"Do not be alarmed," the man says robotically. "My name is Data. I am Mr. Grey's butler."

Oh. My heart stops beating frantically. Well, it keeps beating, just not as frantically as before. I'm calming down.

"Why are you wearing that outfit?" I say.

"This is my Starfleet uniform, Miss Steal," he says.

"Starfleet? Is that like NASA?"

"Your comparison is not one of equivalency," he says.

He must register my look of bewilderment, because he adds, "Surely you are familiar with *Star Trek*?"

I shake my head. "I'm not big into science fiction."

He sighs, and relaxes his entire body. "Thank God," he says, his voice now sounding closer to a normal person's. "You can just call me Brent."

"I'm sorry," I say. "I still don't understand . . ."

"I'm an actor, Miss Steal. Or I was," he says wistfully. "I played an android named 'Data' on *Star Trek: The Next Generation* for many years. Afterward, directors weren't exactly lining up around the block to cast someone whose best-known work is playing basically a robot. Mr. Grey found me working at a Saturn dealership in Beverly Hills, and asked me to come work for him—as his 'android butler.' He apparently wanted a real android, but I was as close as he could get."

I shake my head. "That's tragic. I can't imagine working as a car salesman. Especially one who sells Saturns."

"Oh, the money wasn't bad, Miss Steal," Brent says. "But I did get tired of saying, 'Not only is this model fully functional, it's also fully loaded.' Even if I have to wear this olive-green bodysuit and dye my hair black, working for Mr. Grey pays much, much better. As I'm sure you're aware."

"Mr. Grey doesn't pay me anything," I say defensively. *Unless you count the iPad, and the Hotmail account, and him buying Walmart and Washington State University.* "I'm not a prostitute."

"Oh," Brent says. "I'm sorry. I just assumed . . ."

Oh no. This is what Earl meant when he said he doesn't "do the girlfriend thing." He doesn't have girlfriends, because he pays women to dress up as elves and magicians and whatever else and get spanked and screwed in his Dorm Room of Doom.

"I have to go," I say, sliding past Brent. I change into my own clothes and run from Earl Grey's apartment in tears as his weird android butler watches me, unable to compute my emotions with his circuit board brain.

Chapter Fifteen

I ORDER A GREEN TEA at the Starbucks across the street from Earl Grey's apartment. I pull my phone out and call Kathleen.

She answers after one ring. "Anna!"

"It's me," I say glumly.

"Are you okay?" she asks. It doesn't sound like she's as angry with me as her text messages indicated.

"Yes. No. I don't know," I say.

"Did that control freak kidnap you? Where did he take you?"

I sigh. "To his apartment."

"I'll come pick you up, girl," she says, sensing my dour mood.

"Would you?" I say. "I'm at the Starbucks in Seattle."

"Cool. Hang tight—I'll be there in forty-five minutes or so."

I thank Kathleen and end the call. Now I'm stuck in this coffee shop with nothing to do . . . Should I turn the iPad on? I took it from the apartment, probably against my better judgment. But it's an iPad. C'mon. Who would turn down a free iPad?

I start it up and look it over. It's loaded with tons of apps, including Words With Friends, Angry Birds, and . . . Mail. *Do I dare open it? What could it hurt?* I tap the envelope icon and it expands to fill the screen.

From: Earl Grey <earlgrey50@hotmail.com>
Subject: Your New iPad
Date: May 22 6:49 AM
To: Anna Steal <annasteal@hotmail.com>

Dear Miss Steal—

I hope you slept well. It sure as hell sounded like it! How do you not wake yourself up with your own snoring?!!! Ha ha, j/k. But not really kidding.

Anyway, let me know if you need anything!

Earl Grey
CEO, The Earl Grey Corporation

It's not the only e-mail in my inbox from Earl. There's a new e-mail, dated five minutes ago.

From: Earl Grey <earlgrey50@hotmail.com>
Subject: Baby?
Date: May 22 10:56 AM
To: Anna Steal <annasteal@hotmail.com>

Dear Miss Steal—

Data contacted me and said that you were compelled to leave the apartment most unexpectedly. Is everything okay?

Earl Grey
CEO, The Earl Grey Corporation

P.S. I tried calling your phone, but it went straight to voicemail (it was either off, or you were talking on it?). I'm buying you a second cell phone, just to field my calls exclusively. Don't argue with me, Anna.

Uh-oh. What do I do? I start composing a response . . .

_____

From: Anna Steal <annasteal@hotmail.com>
Subject: RE: Baby?
Date: May 22 11:05 AM
To: Earl Grey <earlgrey50@hotmail.com>

I did leave, yes. And I was on the phone. Not that it's any
of your business.

I am not one of your LARPers. Or should I say "whores"?

Anna

_____

I tap "send" and then close the Mail app. *That'll show the rich bastard.*

I open the Words With Friends app.

There's a small avatar of Earl Grey. I tap on it, and it brings up a new screen: "Earl Grey has invited you to play a game. Would you like to accept?"

Do I accept? I have time to kill. It's an easy enough game, and one that I've played before on my mom's iPad. You're given seven letters, each with a different point value, and must place them on the board by connecting them with at least one letter of a word that the other player has spelled. For every letter you use, you get a new one in the next round. Perhaps I can vent some frustration at Earl Grey through the game.

I tap "yes." I'll play, if only to beat him and show him he's not as smart and clever as he thinks he is. Earl has played the first word: "KINK." Of course.

I look at the letters available to me. Hmmmm . . . I move four letters to the board, spelling "PRICK" off one of his Ks. His move.

Almost immediately, I receive a notice that he has played. His word? "PRICKS." *Damn! Bastard!* He just added an "S" to the end of my word. It's a legal move, but one only a prick who wants to piggyback off someone else's hard work would do.

I spell "CHEAP" off of the "C." Because he's a cheap prick, if he's going to just add "S" to the end of every word I spell.

He plays "HO." *Oh, hell no.*

I turn the iPad off. *The nerve of that man!* I head to the women's restroom to fix my hair, which I can feel is out of control again. I should have tamed it before I left Earl Grey's apartment, but I was in such a hurry to get out of his little whorehouse that I didn't even put on my underwear— I couldn't find them. He'll probably cook them up for dinner or something. What a creep.

I lock the door behind me and stare at myself in the mirror. What does Earl Grey see in me? I'm so plain; I don't wear any makeup. My skin is as pale as Steve Jobs' corpse.

"Anna," a voice says from the closed stall behind me. It's a voice so hunky that it can only be . . .

"Mr. Grey!" I say, turning my head to find him swinging the door open. The toilet flushes and he zips his pants up. His tousled hair looks more magnificent than ever. And those eyes! They're still gray.

"I'm sorry, Anna. 'Ho' was the only word I could spell," he says. "You should have seen what I had to work with."

I shake my head. "You're unbelievable. You could have spelled 'O–H.'"

"Maybe." He grins. "But you look so cute when you're mad. Come sit with me," he says, opening the door and ushering me out of the women's restroom.

"I'm waiting for someone," I say.

"Until he or she gets here, please sit with me. We need to talk."

Fine. What choice do I have? If I don't sit with him, he'll just send a text and buy Starbucks, and have every chair removed except for the ones at his table.

We sit down together. If he can tell I'm drinking green tea instead of Earl Grey tea, he doesn't let on.

Earl clears his throat wickedly. "So, Anna, you think that I think you're a hooker."

"Your butler seemed to think so," I say. "Have you paid other girls for sex?"

He sighs. "That's a very narrow-minded way to look at what I do. It's not easy to find beautiful women who will LARP with me and let me have my way sexually with them. Do I have to pay them sometimes? Yes."

"I knew it. I think we're done here," I say.

I start to rise out of my chair, but he grabs my wrist. "Please hear me out, Anna."

I sit back down. "Fine. Talk."

"I don't expect you to understand. I'm a complicated man, Anna. I have fifty shames. Some of them you already know, such as my intense mancrush on Tom Cruise or the fact that I shop at Walmart. But I have other secret shameful desires that are more . . . sexual in nature."

Oh my.

"Like I told you, I'm into kinky, weird games. You haven't even begun to scratch the surface. Perhaps it's for the best that you leave me. If paying women for erotically charged role-playing sessions bothers you, you could never handle some of the things I'm into. For what it's worth, Anna, the LARPers are all in the past now. I quit buying women the moment I met you. I'm a changed man."

"You'd just rather buy extravagantly expensive things for me instead of throw actual money at me," I say.

"Exactly," he says. "Last night was the first time I've ever had 'vanilla' sex without getting dressed up and doing a role-playing scene. I didn't have to pretend you were a captive orc princess in order to get off. I don't know what you're doing to me, Anna."

My heart skips a beat. "That's incredibly romantic," I say, radiating joy. Maybe things can work out for us after all.

Just then, the door swings open and Kathleen steps into Starbucks. With Jin.

Gulp.

Chapter Sixteen

JIN STANDS OFF TO ONE SIDE behind Kathleen. He can't seriously be ready for another fight, not after what happened at Eclipse. Earl, for his part, remains seated. He's always so cool under pressure. But then again, he's not the one who ended up in the hospital after their last meeting.

"Are you ready to go?" Kathleen says, the anger resonating in her voice. She's not happy that I'm sitting here with Earl. I can't blame her. I need to diffuse the situation before any more testicles get crushed.

"I think I need to leave," I say to Earl.

"I'm not going to try to stop you, Anna," he says.

Wait—Earl Grey is just going to let me go? Without a fight? It doesn't sound like him at all. "Can you guys wait in the car? I'll be right out," I tell Jin and Kathleen.

"Five minutes," Jin says. "Let's go, Kathleen."

They leave, and I'm alone again with Earl.

"So you would let me walk out of here? What gives?"

"I'm used to it by now," he says. *Oh no.* Emo Earl is back. "Everyone in my life leaves me. First, my addict mother. Then my adoptive parents, who abandoned me into foster care. Then Suzy, my girlfriend in the sixth grade, whose parents moved, taking her with them to a faraway school in

Cedar Rapids. Then Ken Griffey Jr. left the Mariners in 2000 to play for the Cincinnati Reds. And now you're leaving me, Anna."

The sadness is unbearable! His gray puppy-dog eyes are too much. "I don't want to leave you," I say.

"Then don't."

"But my friends . . ."

He nods. "I need you, Anna. But I'm not going to make you choose between your friends and me. That wouldn't be fair."

"Thank you. That's very generous of you."

"I can be kind," he says, "when I want to be." His smile is back! Oh, how I missed it. He rises from the table and embraces me in a hug. He licks my cheek from my jawline up to my temple, and back down. We kiss passionately, each of us eager for sweet tongue meat. We break our kiss before one of us swallows the other's tongue. I, for one, have choked enough over the past few days.

"I'll talk to you later this week," I say.

"I'll hump you later this week," he replies.

The car ride back to Portland takes forever. We ride in silence for a long time, before I finally break the ice. "I'm sorry, guys."

I'm in the backseat, and Kathleen is driving. Jin is in the front passenger seat. He looks at me in the rearview mirror, and I see the anger in his green eyes. I also see the worry.

"I'm just glad you're okay," he says.

"Of course I'm okay," I say. "How are your . . . um . . ."

"My *cojones*? My nuts? My wedding tackle?" he says. "Not good. One had to be amputated."

Oh no! "What will you do?"

"What can I do, Anna? I'm not happy about it, but what's done is done. I was drunk; I let my anger get the better of me. I strayed from the brony code of friendship and kindness."

"You did what you thought was right," I say. "You were just looking out for me."

"Let me tell you a story," Jin says. "In the second part of the series premiere of *My Little Pony: Friendship Is Magic*, the ponies confront an angry manticore who is blocking their path. While the other ponies want to fight the beast, Fluttershy calmly approaches it and finds a thorn stuck in its paw. She shows the manticore kindness, instead of anger. After she removes the thorn, the manticore lets the ponies pass.

"If I had been more like Fluttershy and approached your boyfriend with kindness instead of threats, I might have both my testicles today," he says. I don't know what the hell a "manticore" is, but I get the point of his story: Jin was mad about a thorn stuck in his paw. Or something.

He diverts his gaze from the rearview mirror and looks out the window. "I cast shame on the house of bronydom that day. I haven't been able to show my muzzle on Pony-Expression.net since then," he says, his voice full of longing and regret.

There's an awkward pause in the conversation.

"So, uh, what's going on between you and this Earl Grey?" Kathleen asks. Jin visibly tenses up at Earl's name.

"I don't know," I say. "He says he doesn't 'do' the girl-friend thing."

"So you're not dating? He's just whisking you around the Pacific Northwest in his helicopter and buying up every-thing in his path?" Kathleen says.

"Kind of," I say. I don't know how much I want to say about the Dorm Room of Doom. I'm dying to talk about it with Kathleen, but not with Jin in the car.

"He sounds like a real winner," Jin says.

"I just want you guys to give him a chance," I say.

"If he hurts you . . ." Jin's voice trails off.

"Getting hurt is one of the risks of any relationship," I say. *Except in this relationship, I might get tied to a Segway and pushed into traffic one day, all in the name of erotic live-action role playing.* The thought of Earl Grey tying me up makes my womb grow needy with want.

"I killed the story on him for *Boardroom Hotties,*" Kathleen says. "I don't want to give this guy free press. Whatever hap-pens, just know that we have your back, okay?"

I'm surprised she's driving; this is literally the longest I've ever seen her go without taking a drink or throwing up. "Thanks," I say. "It's nice to see you sober for a change."

She laughs. "Oh, I'm totally wasted right now," she says.

"Yeah," Jin adds. "We've been butt chugging."

"Do I want to know what that is?"

"Hell yes," Kathleen says. "First, soak a tampon in vodka. And then—"

"Thanks," I say. "I get the picture."

"It burns, but the alcohol's supposed to enter your bloodstream faster," Kathleen says.

It doesn't sound pleasant or safe. And she shouldn't be driving. "Pull off the road. I'll take over the wheel," I say. I've never driven before, but at least I'm not drunk.

Kathleen nods, then steers the car straight off the road—and into a ravine! As the car flies down the side of the cliff toward the Pacific Ocean, we scream our last words in unison: "Aaaarrrrrghhhh!"

Chapter Seventeen

KATHLEEN'S VOLVO DIVES into the water headfirst. Jin, Kathleen, and I are trapped inside, sinking to our doom. The car's doors are sealed tight, but it's only a matter of time before the windows shatter under the water pressure and we all drown. We're pretty much screwed. If only Jin was a merman instead of a brony! Kathleen has stopped screaming, but her mouth is still wide open. If we somehow survive this ordeal, I'm taking her to an AA meeting.

"We're trapped," Jin says, putting his weight into opening his door without success. "We're too deep already. The pressure is too strong."

"I'm sorry, I'm sorry," Kathleen mutters in between sobs.

"Let's just try to conserve our oxygen," I say.

"How? Hold our breath? Then we'll just pass out," Jin says.

"Do you have a better idea?" I ask. "I'm open to suggestions."

"Yeah, how about you text your boyfriend and have him come save us," Jin says sarcastically.

It's actually not a bad idea. "Fine," I say. I pull my phone out and call my not-boyfriend.

"Anna!" Earl Grey says. He's safe in Seattle and here I am, halfway between Seattle and Portland and ten thousand leagues under the sea.

"Hey," I say. The sound of his voice is so dreamy that I temporarily forget what I was calling him about.

"Are you okay? Did you make it back to Portland?"

"Not exactly," I say. The car finally hits the ocean floor. The clock is ticking.

"Are you in trouble?"

"Yes," I say, a little embarrassed. I'm always getting into trouble and asking Earl to save me. As if he doesn't have anything better to do with his day! "I'm kind of stuck in a car on the bottom of the ocean with Kathleen and Jin."

"I'll be there soon," he says. "Hold tight. Whatever you do, don't die."

"Okay," I say. I'm not sure if that's the sort of thing you can promise a lover, but I'll do my best.

I hang up the phone. "He's on his way," I tell Kathleen and Jin.

Two hours later, we're back on dry land. Kathleen's Volvo is totaled. We survived the accident, thanks to Earl Grey, who drained the Pacific Ocean to save us.

Earl drapes his jacket around me. He's dressed in his button-down shirt and smiley-face tie again, and looks as handsome and dashing as ever. I want him to bend me over and take me on the beach, but it would be kind of awkward with Kathleen and Jin sitting in his helicopter waiting for us.

"You're one lucky girl," Earl says.

"I'm the luckiest girl," I say. "I have you."

He shakes his head. "You never cease to amaze me, Anna."

"I shouldn't have left you," I say, lowering my head. I don't want to see the disappointment in his eyes.

He puts a hand under my chin and gently tilts my face up toward him. "It's okay," he says, his eyes and voice tender and forgiving. "It's okay."

I begin crying. The tears flow quick and fast, like it's raining. Oh, wait—it is raining. I guess I'm not crying after all.

"Let me fly you guys back to Portland before this storm picks up," he says, kissing me on my forehead. We get back on the helicopter. Kathleen and Jin are already passed out, thanks to the alcohol-soaked tampons in their butts.

We begin the flight to Portland in silence. After everything we've been through, the quiet is nice for a change. Even my inner guidette shuts her trap for once. It's during this moment of Zen that I feel something kick in my stomach. OMG. I don't remember eating a baby. This can only mean one thing: I'm pregnant—pregnant with Earl Grey's baby!

Chapter Eighteen

I'M ALONE IN THE HELICOPTER with Earl, and we're headed back to Seattle after dropping off Kathleen and Jin. Thankfully, they didn't put up an argument when I told them I was flying back with Earl. After what happened today, I realized what a mistake it was for me to leave him. A near-death experience was all it took for me to see how much I need Earl Grey. According to him, he's the one who needs me. Maybe we need each other? It sounds like the basis for a completely normal, healthy relationship to me.

"I'm kind of glad you crashed into the ocean," Earl says.

"And why is that, Mr. Grey?"

"Because I'm throwing a masked charity ball tonight, and I'd love for you to come with me."

"You know how I love coming with you," I say, grinning.

"Excellent. Then it's all set. We just need to get back to my apartment, change into something more formal, and we'll be off to the ball."

We're on our way to the charity fund-raiser, which is being held inside the restaurant at the top of the Space Needle.

I'm wearing a short black dress from Earl's closet. He says he had Data buy it just for me, though his wardrobe has more women's clothing than men's. I'm also wearing eyeliner and makeup, which Earl "had Data buy" for me too.

Earl is dressed as impeccably as ever, except he has swapped his smiley-face tie for a more formal tie with hundred-dollar bills printed on it. "This tie cost more than the money printed on the fabric, if you can believe it," he says to me in the Space Needle elevator.

"I can believe it," I say. Hardly anything he says or does shocks me anymore.

Earl Grey looks stunning. I want to stop the elevator and space out on his needle . . . but there are three other sharp-dressed couples on their way to the charity fund-raiser in the elevator with us.

"Anna, you are looking particularly gorgeous tonight," Earl says.

I blush. "Stop," I whisper. "There are other people in here . . ."

"Don't be such a prude," he says. "Hand me your panties."

No one looks at us, but they had to have heard him. Still, I do as I'm told. I slip my panties off under my dress and step out of them. I hand them to Earl.

"Thank you," he says. He leans over my neck and whispers into my ear, "I'm going to get you so wet that everyone in here drowns."

Oh my.

Fortunately, Earl doesn't have a chance to make good on his promise, as the elevator stops. "Another time," I say.

We step off the elevator. The view of the city from the top of the Space Needle is marvelous. The room rotates to give diners at the restaurant a full 360-degree view of Seattle. It normally takes an hour to go around once, but Earl says he had them speed it up so it only takes ten minutes. It's quite extraordinary. I have to remember not to drink too much, because I don't want it spinning in more than one direction.

Earl hands me a piggy mask with a silver ribbon to hold it on. "It's a masked ball," he says. Instead of a pig nose and ears, his mask has a cute lil' mouse nose and ears. We slip them on, covering the top halves of our faces. I can still see Earl's gray eyes. *Oh, we're going to have fun tonight.*

"Would you like to play a game?" he says.

"It depends who I'm playing against."

"Yourself," he says. He produces an impossibly large, rounded red die from his pocket and shows it off to me in the palm of his hand. It's unlike any die I've ever seen in my life.

"What is that?"

"A D-sixty-nine," he says. He must see the look of confusion on my face, because he adds, "A sixty-nine-sided die."

Woah. "I thought you didn't gamble."

"I don't," he says. "Many role-playing games, including BDSM, utilize polyhedral dice to guide the action."

"And just what am I supposed to do with it?"

He smiles. "Isn't it obvious? Slip it inside you, and see how long you can hold it in for."

"Inside me? You mean, inside my—"

He nods.

My inner guidette is hesitant, but I take the die anyway. It's slightly smaller than a golf ball. I slip off into the ladies' room next to the elevator, and then return after doing the deed.

"It's in," I say.

He smiles. "Game on."

Paparazzi surround us once we enter the event space, snapping photos of us together. The lights are blinding. Earl grabs my hand and leads me through the pack of vultures. "You're going to be all over TMZ tomorrow, baby," he says, smiling. "I don't think the press has ever photographed me with a woman who has a sixty-nine-sided die inside her . . ."

"Have they snapped pictures of you with women who aren't carrying dice inside them?" I ask.

"No," he says flatly.

I quickly change the subject. "So you set this whole fundraiser up. What's it benefitting?"

"It's to raise awareness of the dangers of drunk diving," he says matter-of-factly.

"Drunk . . . *diving*?"

"Yes," he says.

"Surely you mean drunk *driving*," I say. "Like my roommate

who almost killed me today." Though we did end up drunk diving, albeit unintentionally. In a car.

Earl shakes his head. "When you see the presentation I give, I'm almost certain you'll be persuaded. Facts don't lie."

As we walk through the room, Earl introduces me to the other guests. There have to be at least five hundred attendees, all wearing animal masks. There's no way I'll even remember their names in the morning. If I see anyone on the street in the morning, will I recognize them?

Earl leads us to a table set up facing the rest of the room. A spotlight turns on him and someone hands him a microphone. I duck out of the light.

When he talks, his voice booms over the PA system. "Welcome, friends, to our annual charity ball!"

The crowd claps wildly for him. "I hope you enjoy the program we've put together for you this evening. The waiters are beginning to bring around the food right now, so don't wait for me to finish blabbing before you start eating."

There's polite laughter. I shift nervously in my chair. The die stashed inside my body doesn't hurt, but I can definitely tell it's there. It takes all my concentration and muscle skills not to let it slip out.

"We're going to start the charity auction soon, and I do hope you'll open up your hearts—and wallets—for us, because it's all for a good cause: to raise awareness of drunk diving.

"Folks, this is a very serious issue. I'm about to read off some statistics that, frankly, shocked me like a car battery hooked up to my nipples.

"Did you know that alcohol is involved in almost fifty percent of the nearly forty thousand diving accidents every year? Every minute, one person in this country is killed in a drunk diving accident. You may think that this doesn't affect you, but think again: one in three people will be involved in an alcohol-related diving accident in their lifetime."

He continues with the facts and figures for over an hour. By the time he wraps his speech up, the waiters are serving dessert. Thank God we didn't wait to eat until he was finished. "But enough with the grim statistics," Earl says. "Who's ready to start the auction?"

Chapter Nineteen

A FAST-TALKING AUCTIONEER takes the microphone from Earl and launches into the bidding rules. Earl sits down. "That was a moving speech," I tell him.

"Thank you," he says, kissing me on the cheek. Well, sort of on the cheek, and partly on the piggy mask.

The crowd cheers. For a second, I think it's because of us kissing, but then I hear the words "Sold! Fifteen thousand dollars" over the PA system. Someone just bought the first edition of *A Shore Thing*, which I made Earl put up for auction since I couldn't accept such an extravagant gift.

"You're doing so much good in the world, Mr. Grey," I tell him.

"It's to balance out the cruelty in my own heart," he says grimly.

I don't say anything, because there's no use arguing with Earl Grey when he's PMSing.

The next item up for bid is a fantasy vacation suite in Hawaii. Without thinking, I raise my hand and scream, "A billion dollars."

The crowd oooohs. The auctioneer is stunned speechless for a moment.

"Going once . . . twice . . . sold," the auctioneer says, "to the young woman in the pig mask."

I look at Earl, whose gray eyes are burning with anger beneath his mouse mask.

"What?" I say to him. "I've always wanted to go to Hawaii."

"Where did you get a billion dollars?" he asks.

Uh-oh. "Are we using real money? I thought we were using Monopoly money."

"No, Anna," he says, his voice quiet. "We're using real money here. I guess I'll have to lend you the billion dollars."

"Thanks," I say sheepishly. *Oops.*

"You do know, however, that the fantasy suite in Hawaii that was auctioned off is one that I own," he says.

"Oh. I didn't know that."

He shakes his head. "What am I ever going to do with you, Anna Steal?"

I have no idea. I'm thinking the same thing about him.

❧

The auction is over, and Earl is slow dancing with me on the dance floor. The house band, the Icy Dragons, is dutifully playing a faithful cover version of "Every Rose Has Its Thorn" at Earl's request. His anger has dissipated, though he says he will probably have to liquidate one or two companies or move a few thousand jobs overseas to pay the billion dollars I owe to the drunk diving charity.

"I'm sorry," I say. "It must have been all the alcohol."

"You haven't been drinking, Anna," he says.

"Then maybe the pot," I say.

"You haven't been smoking pot, either," he says. "It doesn't matter. What's done is done."

Earl is an expert dancer, and guides me around the dance floor with grace. "Where did you learn to dance like this?" I ask him.

"I was on *Dancing with the Stars* once," he says.

"That's so cool," I say.

"I lost in the final round to Nicholas Sparks."

"Is there anything that man can't do?"

"Toss a salad," Earl says gravely.

His body feels good close to me.

"You look so sexy in your mask," he says. "I can't wait to get you home and make you squeal like a pig."

"Thanks," I say. "I think."

"What do you say we make our way to the men's restroom? I don't think I can wait until we leave to have my way with you, Anna," he whispers in my ear.

I smile. "The bathroom? Is that sanitary?"

"Of course. You just have to use a wide stance," he says.

The band finishes the song, and most of the couples exit the dance floor for a breather. "It's just about half past ten. How about we speed things up a bit?" the long-haired male lead singer says as the band launches into a fast-paced rendition of "It's Raining Men."

"I love this song!" I say.

"Me too," Earl says. "What do you say we stick around on the dance floor and I show you some of the moves I learned on *Dancing with the Stars*?"

"I'm kind of clumsy," I say. "I can barely keep up when we're just slow dancing."

"Don't worry so much," he says. "You need to forget your inhibitions and just let yourself go."

"Well, if you insist . . ."

He smiles. "Yes, Anna, I insist."

A handful of dancers hit the hardwood floor. Women are throwing their hands up in the air. Earl Grey, meanwhile, begins twirling me around in circles. I try not to throw up as the world spins around me. Add this to the steady rotation of the entire restaurant inside the Space Needle, and I feel even sicker—

The band's lead singer screams passionately into the microphone as Earl tosses me into the air and catches me. It's not raining men—it's raining Anna Steal!

I find my footing back on the ground, but Earl slides me under his legs and pulls me back up. Suddenly, my feet are off the ground! As if the room wasn't spinning enough as it was, now Earl Grey is swinging me through the air by my arms. If something doesn't stop spinning soon it's going to be raining chunks.

"Hallelujah!" the singer shouts. "It's raining m—"

There's a loud thunk. Earl brings me to an abrupt stop and catches me in his arms. I didn't throw up. Thank my inner guidette! I notice that the musicians have stopped playing, though, and Earl Grey is staring wide-eyed at the

Icy Dragons' lead singer, who is lying on his back, knocked out cold. With horror, I spot a sixty-nine-sided die on the floor next to his unconscious body.

Gulp.

Chapter Twenty

I BOARD EARL GREY'S BOAT. It's one of those ridiculously large yachts, like in a rap video. We're about to cross the Pacific Ocean, which has since been filled back up with rainwater since Earl drained it to save me. It's amazing how Mother Nature can repair herself after we damage her. We'll soon be en route to our fantasy Hawaiian suite, only a day after the horrible incident at the Space Needle. Earl thought I might need the vacation now, as I've been a little shaken up after almost killing the lead singer of the Icy Dragons.

After boarding the boat, the first thing I do is throw my arms in the air and yell, "I'm on a boat, motherfu—"

Earl cuts me off by raising a finger to his mouth and shushing me. He points to a sign that reads: PLEASE, FOR THE SAKE OF OTHER PASSENGERS' SANITY, NO "I'M ON A BOAT" REFERENCES. THANK YOU FOR YOUR COOPERATION.

Oh. Drats.

There's another sign just below that one that answers my next question: YOU ARE NOT THE KING OF THE WORLD, JACK.

"So I can't say 'I'm on a boat' *or* do any *Titanic* impressions? What are we supposed to do on a five-hour boat ride?"

"I think that's obvious," Earl says wickedly.

I smile. Oh yeah. Here we go.

"Fish," he says.

I frown. Fish? Really? "What kind of fishing?"

"Tuna," he says, smiling again. He winks at me.

"Ew," I say. "Was that supposed to be sexy?"

"It was supposed to be. My dirty talk doesn't turn you on?"

I shake my head. "Sometimes. But comparing a woman's vagina to a fish is unacceptable."

"What if I said 'goldfish'? Goldfish are colorful and uniquely beautiful. Like you, my dearest Anna."

I shake my head again. "Just stop. No fish."

"Okay, then what did you have in mind?"

"Drop the double entendres and let's move on to another F-word."

"Oh, Anna," he says. "I thought you'd never ask. Food it is, then! Let's go eat in the dining hall."

It wasn't the F-word I had in mind, of course (it was actually two F-words: friending and Facebook), but it works. I'm hungry. Plus I don't even have a Facebook account.

<hr />

The boat is now sailing on the open water. We sit down at a table in the boat's dining room, which turns out to be an Olive Garden. "I hope you like Italian food, Anna. Olive Garden is my favorite," Earl says as a waiter drops off two menus for us.

What do I say? I mean, yes, I love Italian food . . . but I don't know anyone who would mistake Olive Garden for real Italian food. "I like the breadsticks," I say cheerfully.

He laughs. "You can be honest, Anna."

Okay, if he wants to hear it . . . "I think Olive Garden noodles taste like microwaved plastic spoons," I say. "And don't get me started on their clumpy sauce. They should change their name to 'Shitaly.'"

Earl gazes at me. I'm sure he's going to toss me off the boat like chum for a shark. Instead, he just smiles. "I couldn't agree more. And that's why I love it. It's another of my fifty shames, Anna."

Wow. He's bearing his soul to me. This is deep.

"You're a strange man, Mr. Grey."

"Just wait until we get to Hawaii," he says. "You have no idea how strange I am."

The waiter returns, and Earl orders two of everything on the menu. I'm beginning to think his relationship with food is a little screwed up. It's a miracle that he's in shape and has washboard abs. If I ate like he did, I would need liposuction once a week. He laughs when I tell him this.

"Oh, Anna," he says. "If I waited a full week to have liposuction, there's no way my abs would look like this. I have a doctor come in and suck out my fat every Monday and Thursday."

"Do you think that's healthy?"

"It can't hurt," he says.

I'm still unsure. "I've heard stories of people dying or being seriously injured due to cosmetic surgery."

"Oh Anna, it's not surgery; it's a new procedure called 'manual suction.' A doctor comes over and literally sucks the fat off me twice a week using a Dirt Devil."

It's useless to argue with the great and mighty Earl Grey— if he can buy it, then it has to be good, right?

I am glad that he's revealing more of himself to me. No matter how shameful his activities are (eating at Olive Garden, shopping at Walmart, paying for sex), they don't discourage me from getting close to him. If anything, I feel a stronger connection to him with each new revelation. Is there a point where I will be overwhelmed and unable to handle his secrets? Is there something so shameful that it will cause me to leave him forever? How dark can things get?

After we finish eating, I retire to the upper deck to sunbathe. I've brought all 1,200 pages (or whatever) of Earl's quiz to read through again. Earl lounges on one of the lower decks, buying and selling companies on his Black-Berry.

～⌒⊃

It takes me over three hours to read through the quiz for the second time. When I'm finished, I pick up my iPad and sit under an umbrella so I can have some shade while typing. I start the e-mail app.

From: Anna Steal <annasteal@hotmail.com>
Subject: Let's Talk About Us
Date: May 23 5:05 PM
To: Earl Grey <earlgrey50@hotmail.com>

So I revisited the quiz. And I still think you're insane if you want me to fill it out.

Let's begin with the obtrusive questions about "hard limits." Am I interested in "acts involving urine, feces, fireworks, golf clubs, or animals"? Um, no. Disgusting.

Also: The questions about what parts of my life I would let you control? Over the line. No way am I going to let you tell me what to eat, or when to eat it. Is this a romantic relationship or Weight Watchers?

Anna

Less than a minute later, there's a reply from Earl Grey. Somebody clearly wasn't busy enough.

From: Earl Grey <earlgrey50@hotmail.com>
Subject: Okay
Date: May 23 5:06 PM
To: Anna Steal <annasteal@hotmail.com>

Dear Miss Steal—

The hard limits are negotiable. I find that it's always best to discuss these things in advance, however, so that you don't wake up one morning with a Cleveland steamer on your chest and wonder what you've gotten yourself into.

The dietary restrictions are also up for negotiation. You don't have to eat from a prescribed list of foods all the time if that's not what you want. We can compromise. For instance, I can provide a list of foods to be eaten as snacks (baby carrots?).

Earl Grey
CEO, The Earl Grey Corporation

I e-mail back that baby carrots might be an acceptable compromise. After I hit "send," I put the iPad into sleep mode and set it aside. I recline in the lawn chair and close my eyes, ready to nap under the shade. Before I can drift off, however, something tickles my face. I open my eyes and what I come face-to-face with is definitely not a baby carrot.

I glance up at Earl's grinning face. "We've got about an hour left," he says. "I have an F-word in mind that can keep us occupied . . ."

After we run through a fire drill, Earl and I stroll to the front of the yacht to get a good view of our destination. I haven't told him about the baby yet. He's going to blame me for it; I need to wait for the right time to tell him he's going to be a father.

"Have you ever been to Hawaii?" he asks me.

I shake my head. "I've never left the United States." In the distance, I can see the sun setting over the Pacific Ocean. In the middle of the great big blue sea, a series of islands covered in beautiful lush green vegetation rises majestically.

"I can't believe you have a place in Hawaii," I say.

"I have an *island* in Hawaii," he says.

Swoon.

Chapter Twenty-one

EARL GREY RUNS THE BOAT onto the beach and we hop out. We're not dressed for the beach: he's in his suit and I've changed into a sundress. It hardly matters, because the beach is deserted.

"Where is everybody?" I say.

"This is a private beach," he says. "Just you, me, and a hundred paparazzi in boats and helicopters trying to get a glimpse of Earl Grey sunbathing nude."

"You tan in the buff?"

"Does that surprise you, Anna?"

"A little. But only because you're so pale."

He shrugs. "It's been a few weeks since I've been here," he says. "C'mon."

Earl grabs my hand and leads me to a cabin on the edge of the beach, where the sand meets the tropical forest. We step inside the cabin and he turns the lights on. *Wow.* What a place. There are so many things, like couches and chairs and tables. Everything is very tastefully done up in white and earth tones. The walls are lined with black velvet paintings of the greatest figures of the past century, including Elvis Presley, Steve Jobs, Usher, Jeff Foxworthy, George W. Bush, and Oprah Winfrey. "It's beautiful," I say.

"Of course the cabin is beautiful," he says. "I decorated it."

"You can decorate me," I say. *Damn my potty mouth!*

Earl raises an eyebrow. "The things that come out of your mouth," he says amusedly.

"The things that come in my mouth," I reply.

"That's it," he says, loosening his tie. "I think you need to be disciplined for being so naughty."

Uh-oh. What does he have in mind?

"We're a ways away from your Dorm Room of Doom, so I'm not scared," I say.

He cocks an eye. "What did you call it?"

Gulp. "Room of Doom. Why? What do you think I said?"

He shakes his head. "Nevermind," he says, removing his smiley-face tie. He pulls me by my wrist into the cabin's bedroom.

"Take off your clothes," he orders me.

"Yes, Mr. Grey," I say. I'm not sure what he has in mind, but I start stripping. I hope he's not mad about the crack about his Room of Doom. When I'm down to my panties and bra, I realize he hasn't removed anything except for his tie.

"Not joining me?" I say.

He shakes his head. "I'm not joining you. I'm disciplining you. Now finish undressing and lie down on the bed."

I do as instructed. I'm lying on my back, naked, my legs bent at the knees and ready to receive Earl. Suddenly, his hands are pinning my wrists against the headboard. He's fussing with his tie . . . Wait! He's tied me up! I am spread eagle, naked before him, my arms raised above my head and tied to one of the bedposts.

He steps back and surveys his work. "Nice," he says. "I like seeing you tied up. So helpless, so defenseless . . ."

His sadistic impulses are in full force this evening. It's kind of hot to temporarily give up control to him. He's driving me crazy with anticipation. "Please, Mr. Grey," I pout. "Please use me."

"No whining," he says. "If you do, I will put a ball gag in your mouth."

"Yes, put your balls in my mouth," I say. "I want to eat your balls."

He pauses. "I meant a ball gag, which is a rubber ball," he says.

"Oh," I say disappointedly.

"Hold tight," he says, licking his lips. "I'm going to get something to drink."

I watch him leave the room, his muscular butt visible through his pants. I can hear him opening the refrigerator in the kitchen. He returns, a filled wineglass in his hand.

"I hope you're thirsty," he says, nearing the bed.

He puts it to my mouth, and I sip the carbonated purple drink. It's chilled, and tastes like a cross between grape Kool-Aid and Miller High Life.

He pulls it back. "You can't even buy this anymore, you know," he says.

"It's delicious," I say. "What is it?"

"Four Loko," Earl says. "It has twelve percent alcohol and enough caffeine to wake Paula Deen from a diabetic coma.

It's so powerful that the federal government made them re-formulate it to remove the caffeine and herbs. Thankfully, I have cases of the original formulation stashed here in my wine cellar."

"So it's illegal," I say.

"According to the government," he says. "But this will be our little secret, okay?"

"Okay. Now are we going to have sex?" My lady boner is throbbing in anticipation of his Bilbo Baggins.

"Not yet," he says. "First, I'm going to have a little fun . . ."

Earl drips Four Loko onto my sternum and it pools between my breasts. "Hold still," he says.

"It's cold!" I shriek.

Earl, still fully clothed, bends his head to my chest and begins lapping up the Four Loko with his tongue like a cat drinking from a water bowl.

"How nice does this feel, Anna?" he says, raising his head and looking me in the eyes. My chest is now just sticky instead of wet. I feel some of the cool liquid dripping into my armpits.

"It's . . . kinky," I say. Is it supposed to feel good? When he was licking it up, it tickled. Now I just feel gross.

"You want more," he says, pouring the liquid on my stomach. It trails off into my pubic hair. I can't wait to get into the shower after this is over.

He laps it up again, and this time the tickling sensation is too much. I squirm involuntarily, accidentally bringing my knee up and into his chin. He drops the glass of Four

Loko, spilling it onto the bed. It runs underneath my ass. "Dammit!" I scream.

Earl rolls off me and falls off the bed onto the floor. It's a few moments before he says anything or moves. Then I see a hand on the bed, and he picks himself up. "Dammit? Why did you say 'dammit'? I was the one who was kicked in the face."

"The Four Loko is cold. It ran under my butt," I say. "Sorry."

He shakes his head. "I didn't realize you could kick so hard. You surprise me so much," he says, rubbing his chin. "It's like I learn something new about you every day."

"Maybe it's because we've only known each other for a week," I say.

"There is that." After a pause, he adds, "But let's get back to our little game, shall we?"

"Please," I say. My arms are getting tired and now my butt cheeks are sticking together; I don't know how much longer I can take this. If we ever do get around to the actual sex, perhaps I'll quickly fake an orgasm so I can get to the shower sooner.

He kneels between my legs, and spreads them even farther apart. He's in his suit still, and I can see the Four Loko getting his pants damp. I hope he has a dry cleaner on this island. I'm sure he does—he has everything.

"Now it's time for me to drink *you*, Anna," he says, lying down on the bed and positioning his head between my legs.

"Shoot!" I yell. There's something I forgot, something that's suddenly a very pressing matter.

He looks up at me. "What is it?"

"Well . . ."

"Tell me, Anna. You can tell me anything."

How do I say this delicately? There's no easy way, so I just launch into it. "I was spotting blood this afternoon after all the sexy time over the past few days," I say. "I'm supposed to get my period this week, so I thought I might be getting it early. I wasn't sure. I put a tampon in to be safe." I leave off the part about knowing I'm not on my period because I'm pregnant with his child.

"It's okay, Anna," he says. "I'm no stranger to blood." The way his gray eyes suddenly light up when he says "blood" worries me a little. Like he's thirsty for it . . .

He reaches a hand between my legs and, using his long fingers, grasps the tiny string at my heavenly gates. "Hold still," he says, tugging gently on it. The tampon slides out easily; much to my relief, there's very little blood on it. I should have used a panty liner, but I didn't have any with me. Oh well. No harm done.

Earl tosses the tampon into a short trash can beside the bed. "Now back to business," he says, diving back toward me.

He furrows his brow. He has great, attractive eyebrows that lend themselves to brow furrowing. They're like two animated caterpillars doing the Hokey-Pokey above his gray eyes. "Hold still," he says. "There's something else . . ." He reaches his long fingers back into my womanly chasm and—

"Aha!" he says, relaxing his puzzled look. He tugs gently on something inside me, and slowly draws a yellow hand-kerchief through my mud flaps and into the air. What a trick! He winks at me; I smile back. He's not done, though—he keeps pulling, and a blue one, attached to the first, follows! And then an orange one! He continues pulling, and ends up with a string of twelve handkerchiefs, all tied together. It's the sweetest magic trick anyone has ever done using my Katy Perry. I would clap, but my hands are still tied up above my head.

Earl raises his index finger and smiles wickedly. One more thing! What will he "find" inside me next? I look at him quizzically. No way in hell is he pulling a rabbit out of me . . . He inserts two of his long fingers back inside me and begins feeling along the upper wall of my mantrap. He presses his fingers into an area rich with nerve endings. It feels . . . delicious. "Look what I found," he says, registering the look of pure bliss on my face. "Your G-spot."

For the next fifteen minutes, Earl works on me with his long fingers. The tie keeps my hands held in place firmly above my head, so I can't interfere or guide him. It's maddening yet oh so erotic. I get wetter and wetter the closer I get to climaxing, until I'm certain I will die of dehydration. But I don't die. Instead, my body shudders in one final bout of ecstasy. My climax seems to last for several minutes, to the point I simply can't take it anymore. I collapse, his tie digging deeper into my wrists. I'm exhausted yet fulfilled. Also, my hands may need to be amputated.

"That was . . ." I trail off, unable to complete my sentence. I gaze at him dreamily.

Earl slowly pulls his fingers out of me, and as he does he pulls something else out: a white dove!

"Presto!" he says, cradling the dove in his hand. The bird coos, and then spreads and flaps its wings to shake off my love juice. Earl lets the dove go, smiling as it soars to the heavens and—

—into the ceiling fan. We are both sprayed with feathers. The bird's lifeless and mangled body is thrown against the wall.

"That certainly didn't go as planned," Earl says, stepping off the bed and untying me.

No shit, Sherlock. It occurs to me what an apt metaphor the bird's death is, though: a poor, innocent, virginal white dove clubbed to death by the sadistic ceiling fan. Can Earl and I ever have a normal life together? Or will his dark desires drive him over the edge? It's a question best left for another time. For now, covered in feathers and Four Loko, I sleep.

Chapter Twenty-two

I WAKE UP AGAIN TO AN EMPTY BED. Sunlight streams into the cabin. Where is Earl? I hear the toilet flush and he saunters out of the bathroom. He is completely naked, and his skin seems to sparkle in the sunlight. Just like a—

"Good morning, Anna," he says.

"I thought you'd left me," I say. "No work today?"

He shakes his head. "I called in sick," he says.

Oh no. "Do you feel ill? What's wrong?"

He laughs. "Oh, Anna," he says. "I'm love sick."

Did he just use the L-word? "Are you in love with me, Mr. Grey?"

"Isn't it obvious?" he says. It's hard to concentrate on his words when his James Franco is flopping about between his legs.

My inner guidette hesitates. If he's in love with me, then that begs the question: Am I in love with him? He's so attractive, and so rich—but on the flip side, he's a moody bastard whose fifty shames constantly threaten to overwhelm him and anyone he comes into contact with. It's a lot to process this early in the morning.

"What time is it?" I ask, changing the topic.

He smiles. "It's the dicking hour, baby."

147

~⌒◌

After we have sex three times in a variety of interesting positions, Earl says he has a surprise for me.

"Can I take a shower first?" I ask. I still have feathers stuck to my body.

"Of course," he says. "Mind if I join you?"

We bang twice in the shower, once using a loofah and once completely upside down. After I have my fifth orgasm of the morning, we step out of the shower and towel off. Most of our sex so far has been fairly normal. It pleases me, because I don't have any interest in being caned or Tasered or whatever. But could it ever be enough for the sadistic Earl Grey?

I ask him what the surprise is.

"You'll see," he says, bending me over the sink and doing me again.

⌒◌

After we dress in matching Hawaiian shirts ("aloha shirts" in Hawaii, according to Earl, who is practically a walking and talking Wikipedia), we mount an ATV and cruise through the jungle. Earl instructed me to wear a skirt and leave my panties at the cabin. Sitting behind him, my legs spread around him, with my pubic hair whipping in the wind: This is so perfect.

We stop at a large set of wooden doors that have to be at least a hundred feet tall. They're the only entrance through an enormous wall that seems to run for thousands of feet in either direction.

"What is this?"

Earl presses a button on his keychain and the doors swing open. "Welcome to Triassic Safari," he says.

"Is this like *Jurassic Park*?" I ask. I may have been only a baby when the movie came out, but it's one even I've heard of.

"Mine came first," he says.

"You weren't even ten when the movie came out," I say.

"I had the idea when I was five months old. I didn't have the money and expertise to execute it until a few years ago. Michael Crichton scooped me, but there's one major difference here: my dinosaurs are real," he says.

"And the ones in the movie weren't?"

He shakes his head. "Oh, Anna," he says. "Your sense of humor is what makes you truly beautiful."

I don't think I have a sense of humor, but whatever. He drives us through the gate, which swings closed when we're safely on the other side.

"So are any of your dinosaurs dangerous?" I ask.

"No more dangerous than me," he says.

Uh-oh.

Earl slows the ATV to a halt beside two dinosaurs eating berries and leaves off bushes. The dinosaurs are the size of school buses. They look like gigantic rhinos, except with more horns. One of them is outfitted with a saddle.

"You ready for the ride of your life?" Earl asks me.

"I thought that's what we did earlier." I smirk.

"Touché, Anna. Touché."

We hop off the ATV and approach the dinosaur with the saddle. "These are *Kosmoceratops richardson*," he says. "The world's horniest animals."

"Excuse me?"

"Count the horns, Anna," Earl says. "Fifteen full-sized horns on her head, plus sixteen smaller horns along the ridge of her skull. The horns most likely evolved as a mating display, but much like their cousin, the *Triceratops*, both males and females have similar horns."

Earl puts a hand on the side of the *Kosmoceratops* and pets its scaly blue skin. The animal purrs at his touch.

"She's so cute," I say.

"That's because I splice their DNA with genetic material from kittens," Earl says. He pulls himself up onto the *Kosmoceratops*'s saddle and extends a hand down to me. I take his hand and climb onto the saddle with him, sitting in front this time. Before I know it, I'm riding around Earl Grey's private island on a freaking dinosaur!

"Have you ever had sex on dinosaur-back?" Earl asks, his arms wrapped around me.

Oh my. I shake my head.

His hands crawl up my shirt and he feels my party favors up. My nipples are rock hard again. It's suddenly obvious why he wanted me to wear the skirt and go commando . . .

"Lean forward," he says. I do as I'm told, holding on to the reins of the *Kosmoceratops*. The animal trots gently through the jungle at a leisurely pace, blissfully unaware that two people are getting busy on her back.

Earl hikes my skirt up, exposing my bare bottom to the cool island breeze. If I had any panties on, I would have soaked through them by now. Instead, the saddle has turned into a Slip 'n Slide. I hear the unbuckling of Earl's belt and the unzipping of his pants. I feel the heat radiating off his throbbing wand.

After Earl sheathes himself, he guides me onto his lap. I ride him for the next half hour as the *Kosmoceratops* carries us across the island under the gorgeous midday sun. He wasn't lying when he said it would be the ride of my life.

<hr />

On the helicopter flight back to Seattle later in the evening, Earl finally brings up the one topic we avoided while on the island. "You read through the quiz again on the boat, but still haven't filled it out."

Uh-oh. "I know, Mr. Grey."

He pauses. "I don't think it's necessary any longer," he says finally.

"Really?"

"You're not like my other LARPers, Anna," he says. "What we have together is different. It's more like . . ."

"Love?" I say.

"Exactly," he says, beaming at me.

Instead of being reassured about our relationship status, however, I'm worried. Can someone change so completely over the course of a few days? Is that how love works? Maybe if we were in a romantic comedy. To me, it feels more like we're in a tragedy.

"What if you're not the freak, Mr. Grey? What if I'm the freak?"

"Did you like being tied up last night?" he asks.

I shrug. "It was fun, except for the dead bird."

"It's just a taste of what you can expect in the world of erotic live-action role playing," he says. "Except for the dead bird, of course."

"That makes me feel a little better," I say.

"I'd still like to do a BDSM scene with you," he says.

"Fine," I say. Can a role-playing scene get any stranger than any of the other things we've done this week?

Earl shakes his head. "I'm afraid you won't accept me once you see how deviant my tastes are . . ."

"I would prefer to see the real Earl Grey, not the Earl Grey you think I want to see," I say. "You're right—we don't need the quiz. I'm not just some random woman you've met through Craigslist. But I don't want you to think you have to change for me."

Earl stares at me with his gray eyes for what seems like an eternity. "I love you, Anna," he says. "Unconditionally."

He's just too good looking to say no to. I can't quit him, even if I tried. Mostly because he would stalk me to the ends of the earth, but still.

"And I . . ." I know the words, but I've never said them out loud to anyone before. Not even to my family. Earl's eyes are transfixed on me. Instead of giving me the confidence I need, they're making me nervous. *It's okay, Anna. You can do this.* "Mr. Grey . . . Earl . . . I love y—"

Before I can finish my sentence, our helicopter crashes into the Space Needle. Everything goes black.

Chapter Twenty-three

I OPEN MY EYES, and find myself eye level with my mother's bare mammaries. It's like being born and going straight for the teat, only I'm twenty-one and WHAT THE HELL?

"Mom?" I whisper.

She and her husband are standing by my bedside. They are both stark naked. Of course it's because they're nudists, but it still shocks me every time I see them. It makes getting through airport security a breeze, they always joke.

Then what has happened rushes back to me. The helicopter crash. *No!*

"Earl!" I shout.

"Calm down, Anna," my stepfather says. "Earl Grey is fine, but you've been hurt. You're in a hospital."

"The heart monitor, the hospital gown, the hospital bed—now it all makes sense," I say.

"Your father sent you these flowers," my mother says, motioning to a marijuana plant on the nightstand. "The good news is, you're going to make it. Mr. Grey has flown in the best doctors from around the world to treat you."

Celebrity doctor Drew Pinsky enters the room. Since he's one of those doctors too good looking to do something so ordinary as wear a white coat, he's dressed in a tasteful baby-blue button-down shirt with a light-yellow tie. His hair is cropped short and his glasses look like they were designed specifically for his angular face. And his arms! All I can see are his forearms, since his sleeves are rolled up, but RAWR. *He works out.*

"I see our little Cinderella is awake," he says to my mother and stepfather. "Mr. Grey flew me in from Los Angeles to treat you."

"Sleeping Beauty," I correct him.

"Excuse me?" he says.

"The fairy tale where the girl falls asleep after biting the poison apple is 'Sleeping Beauty,' not 'Cinderella,'" I say.

Dr. Drew nods. "Of course. I was just, uh, testing your concussion. Sounds like your brain is functioning normally. Always a good sign." He flashes a penlight into my eyes. "Dilating normally," he says.

Dr. Drew smiles at my mother and stepfather. "Could I have a moment alone with your daughter? I need to run over some of the more confidential information relating to her condition. If you can wait outside, I'll let you know when I'm through." They nod and leave us alone.

"My pupils are dilating. My memory is fine. So am I free to go? Where's Mr. Grey?"

"I sent him home once your family got here," Dr. Drew says. "He stood vigil beside your bed for the past seventy-two hours. And I'd like to keep you under observation at least through the night. You broke several bones in your legs, which we were able to heal using the latest medical technology, but you've been in a medically induced coma to treat the swelling in your brain."

Wow. "I guess I was really messed up," I say. And then it hits me: the baby! Our eyes lock.

He lowers his gaze. "We need to talk about something," he says.

"The baby," I say.

He nods. "The baby is fine. But . . ."

A wave of relief floods over me. "But what?"

"I ran some tests, and your baby is a sadist. Just like his father."

"What? How is that possible?" I ask. Also: it's a baby boy! But also: WTF?

"It's very unusual this early in a pregnancy for a baby to be kicking, but I felt it, and I'm sure you have too," he says.

I nod.

"You're less than a week along. Can you imagine what this baby will do to your insides at nine months?"

Gulp. "What should I do?"

"First: Does Earl Grey know?"

I shake my head. "I just found out myself days before the accident at the Space Needle."

"Talk it over with him," Dr. Drew says. "I'm not saying there isn't any hope, but I just want you to know the risks involved with carrying Earl Grey's baby."

"I don't know if I can talk it over with him," I mutter.

"Relationship problems?"

"Where do I begin?" I say. "As you know, he's a sadist. A controlling, egomaniacal sociopath who treats women as objects to be sexually and psychologically abused."

"That's why he's so attached to his Dungeon Master persona. Role-playing his fantasies is how he handles his sadistic desires. BDSM is a game where he is in total control of himself and the women he invites to play with him. Do you find his antics in the bedroom exciting?"

I sigh. "I do. Sometimes. I mean, I like the idea of an alpha male Dungeon Master tossing me around the bedroom on occasion. But I feel that he's holding back a part of himself around me, like he's too ashamed of his own dark impulses to reveal himself fully . . ."

Just then, there's a knock at the door and Earl steps through. Even though he hasn't slept for days, he still looks as attractive and alert as ever. He's dressed in his gray business suit again, which he wears like a boss. I guess that makes sense, because he *is* a boss. "Knock, knock," he says.

"Mr. Grey!" I scream.

He rushes across the room to me and we greet each other with a long hug that turns into a deep, passionate kiss with his tongue diving down my throat like a seagull lunging for an old french fry on the pavement. That turns into Earl unbuckling his pants, and me untying my hospital gown. "I want to suck your eyeballs," I tell him.

"So, ah, I'll just leave you two alone then," Dr. Drew says, showing himself out.

Earl has stripped his pants and boxers off, and mounts the bed. I am naked underneath him, ready to accept his rigid disco stick. Out of the corner of my eye, I can see that the bathroom door is cracked open slightly. A pair of beady eyes peeks through at us.

"Wait," I say. "I can see you, Dr. Drew."

He steps out of the bathroom. "Oh," he says. "I was just, ah, um, washing my hands before I left. Hospital policy."

Earl stares him down and Dr. Drew quickly retreats out of the room. "I'll just tell your parents to wait out here until you're done," the doctor says, closing the door.

"Now where were we?" Earl says, pressing his body down on me. "Oh, I remember: we were nearing the city limits of Fucksville," he says, thrusting into me as my heart monitor beeps wildly out of control.

After we finish fornicating, we dress and let my mother and stepfather back into the room. Thankfully, I don't have to do any introductions since Earl met them earlier in the day when they first arrived in Seattle. The air is damp with our sweat and our hair is totally JBF, but my mother doesn't say anything. My stepfather has a knowing smirk on his face, but he doesn't say anything either. I mean, like nudists can ever take the moral high ground. It's tough to be judgmental with your balls showing.

Earl says he has to return to work but, really, when does Earl Grey *have* to work? I think he's just trying to give me time alone with my family. After he leaves, my mother says, "So he's a cute one."

I blush.

"A little older than you, but I wouldn't kick him out of a Burger King bathroom, if you know what I mean," she says.

My stepfather just laughs. "For what he's worth, neither would I." His sudden erection says he's not kidding.

"Stop, you guys are embarrassing me," I say.

"We're just glad you've finally met someone," my mother says.

"Thanks," I mutter. What would they say if they knew I was pregnant with Earl Grey's baby? I don't think they would be so happy for me.

They say they contacted Kathleen and Jin and left them several voice messages. I keep waiting for another knock at the door, for Jin and Kathleen to check in on me and bring me flowers and balloons, but they're nowhere to be found. I check my cell phone beside my bed: no messages. Even though I'm here with my family, I've never felt more alone. Possibly because I'm the only one wearing any clothing. Is this how my life together with Earl will be? Me in the hospital, him visiting to sex me up, and my mother and her d-bag husband keeping me company? I stare at the red roses Earl left by my bedside. *Every rose has its thorn* . . .

Chapter Twenty-four

WHEN I'M FINALLY DISCHARGED from the hospital at noon the next day, Earl Grey picks me up in typical Earl Grey fashion: although he's ditched the helicopter (which was totaled in the Space Needle crash), he pulls up at the hospital entrance in a NASCAR stock car. "I'm so glad you're okay," Earl says, greeting me in front of the hospital. He's wearing a racing jumpsuit covered in logos of companies he owns. "I thought I lost you."

I shake my head. "You won't lose me that easily."

He kisses me. It's a deep, long, passionate kiss that seems to last forever, like a low-scoring, tied baseball game that's gone on for forty-seven innings. An ambulance rolls up behind Earl's stock car and the ambulance driver lays on the horn. Apparently, Earl is parked in the emergency room lane. I start to break away from his kiss, but Earl sucks harder at my mouth. Our passion cannot be interrupted by rude ambulance drivers and their honky horns and dying patients!

When we finally part lips, the sun is setting and there is a line of sixteen ambulances backed up behind Earl's stock car. He gives a little wave to the pissed off ambulance drivers, and we hop into his car and speed off into the Seattle traffic.

"So what's the story behind this car?" I ask once we're on the road.

"I could tell you it's a replica of the car Tom Cruise drove in *Days of Thunder*, but that would be a lie," he says. "It's the actual car."

I shake my head. Earl Grey sure has a hard-on for this Tom Cruise guy. "Wow," I say.

"It's okay, you don't have to act impressed," he says. "I'd rather you be impressed by the size of my cock than by the car I drive."

"No problem there, Mr. Grey." I smile. He tilts his head toward me and smiles back. "But keep your eyes on the road, Sir."

"Point taken," he says, turning his attention back to the road.

"Where are we headed?" I ask.

"I've got a surprise for you," he says, speeding into the hills.

⁓

Twenty minutes later, we pull up into the driveway of a secluded mansion overlooking Seattle. The setting sun is beautiful and romantic. "Who lives here?" I ask.

"Eddie Vedder," he says, killing the ignition. "But it's on the market. I thought I'd bring you here and see what you think of it."

We step out of the car. "You want to buy this place?"

"If you like it," he says.

Earl pulls a key out of his pocket and opens the door to the mansion. "Eddie's on tour with Pearl Jam right now, but he lent me a key so we could give it a test drive," he says, smirking wickedly.

We enter the house. Like everything Earl shows me, it's amazing. The bright color scheme, the space-age furniture, the floor-to-ceiling fish tank with naked women swimming in it—just walking through the door, I already know this is where I want to spend the rest of my life. This is where I want to spend the rest of *our* life.

"Did you decorate this place too?" I ask.

Earl nods. "You know it, baby."

"You're so talented," I say. It doesn't seem fair that one man could be so beautiful, and so talented, and so rich, but damn: Earl Grey is the total package. My inner guidette shakes her head. *That's like the fiftieth time you've said that, using nearly the exact same words,* she says. I'm about ready to tell her to go back to styling her poof, when I feel a kick in my abdomen. The baby! It reminds me of Earl's sadism. Is all the money in the world worth putting up with the pain he'll subject me to in order to satisfy his own twisted desires?

Earl takes me on a tour of the mansion. It has sixteen living rooms, a recording studio, a bowling alley with thirty-two lanes, and two and a half bathrooms. "Plus," Earl says, "there's even a guest bedroom for when your parents come to visit."

"Or my friends," I say.

Earl doesn't look happy when I say this, but he nods. "If your friends want to stay, sure," he says. "But Jin will have to sleep in the horse barn out back."

My mouth drops open. "Why do you have to be such an asshole sometimes?"

"I don't know," he says. "I'm sorry. I care about you. Ponyboy just wants to get into your pants. I have to protect what's mine."

"So I'm yours," I say curtly.

"If you want to be, yes," he says. "I've already told you how I feel about you."

And I was going to tell you, until you crashed us into the flipping Space Needle. "What happened to make you this way?" I ask, avoiding the L-word for the moment.

He ignores me. We walk into the Starbucks inside Eddie Vedder's house. Earl orders a Pike Place Roast from the barista, and then looks at me expectantly. "What will you have? Your usual?"

I nod. "Earl Grey. Hot."

After he pays, we take our drinks with us and sit on the patio overlooking Seattle. The sun is still setting. "Is it this beautiful every day in Seattle? I always thought it was supposed to be cloudy and rainy," I say.

Earl laughs wickedly. "That's all part of the city's anti-tourism campaign," he says. "The truth is, it *never* rains in Seattle."

I sip my Earl Grey tea. It's hot, but not as hot as Earl Grey. "You never answered my question," I say. "What happened to you as a child?"

"You want to know why I'm so sadistic. Why I take pleasure in causing pain."

"Yes."

"My father was killed in a drunk diving accident when I was an infant. My mother raised me by herself," he says. "Unfortunately, she was a gambling addict. She practically lived in casinos. In fact, I barely have any memories of her except for a few snippets of her with feathered hair. I remember feeling very lonely.

"When I was four, my mother lost me in a high-stakes poker game to Bill Gates. Mr. Gates brought me to Seattle, but had no interest in being a father to me, this helpless gambler's son. He gave me sixteen billion dollars and set me up with a foster family."

"I had no idea how rough you had it," I say. "Where is your mother now?"

He shakes his head and gazes into the setting sun. "I tried to look her up once, but found out that she died of a gambling overdose."

"That's so heartbreaking," I say.

"Dr. Drew says that when I tie up women and spank them, I'm acting out the anger I feel towards my mother."

"Do you believe that?"

"I don't know," he says. "I was lost for years. I was a marshmallow addict and chocoholic; my grades suffered at school. When I was twelve, a classmate introduced me to AD&D."

"AD&D?"

"Advanced Dungeons and Dragons," he says. "A role-playing game. By pretending to be someone else, I was able to escape my chaotic life. Once I became a Dungeon Master and started orchestrating our scenes, I found that I liked being the one in control. I wasn't at the whim of foster parents or Bill Gates.

"Alas, the good times didn't last forever. As my friends started meeting girls and having sex, they stopped role-playing. My own hormones soon started raging as well. That's when I discovered BDSM—Bards, Dragons, Sorcery, and Magick. Erotic live-action role playing."

"I don't understand why you didn't tell me all of this up-front," I say.

"I told you I have fifty shames," he says. "Role playing is one of them. Things like Nickelback and Olive Garden are others."

"Why do you need to feel ashamed at all?"

"A rich guy like me isn't supposed to enjoy these things," he says. "I'm supposed to drink three-hundred dollar bottles of Pinot Noir and listen to classical music. My pleasures, however, are of the guilty variety. I can't share them with the other rich people at the country club. Feeling shameful is the only way I can reconcile my desires with the pressure to fit into the box society puts its aristocratic class in."

"Can't you just, I don't know, like the things other rich people like? Would that be so hard?"

Earl shakes his head. "We can't choose the things we like any more than we can choose who we love."

"Have you ever had a normal relationship?"

"You're my first," he says. "And, hopefully, my last."

"The way you say that sounds like you're planning to kill me," I mutter.

He laughs. "I would never kill you," he says. "I might pay someone else to, but I would never do it myself."

"That's reassuring."

"It's true. I can't hurt you," he says.

"What if I want you to?"

"Hurt you? Why would you want me to do that?"

"I want you to do your worst. I want to feel the full fury of the sadistic bastard Earl Grey. If you're asking me to move in with you, if you're asking me to love you, I need to know how dark things can get."

He narrows his gray eyes. "You're sure you want to do this," he says.

I nod. I realize my index finger is buried in my nostril up to the second knuckle, and remove it before Earl can admonish me.

He shakes his head. "I would say, 'What am I going to do with you, Anna?' but I know exactly what I'm going to do." He grabs me by the wrist and marches me back to his stock car, then drives like a Cullen toward downtown Seattle. I know what the next stop is: the Dorm Room of Doom. We're finally going to role play.

Chapter Twenty-five

W E'RE BEING FOLLOWED," Earl says, glancing in the
rearview mirror. I look into the passenger-side mirror. There's a solitary pair of headlights closing in on us.

"How do you know they're following us?" I ask. We're on
a two-lane highway en route to Seattle, and there's little
room to pass, thanks to the frequent curves. "Could just be
some asshole tailgating . . ."

Earl shakes his head. "It's the same silver PT Cruiser I
saw earlier when we were heading up to Eddie Vedder's
place. They kept driving when we pulled into the driveway,
so I didn't think twice about it."

"You should have told me," I say.

"And frighten you for no good reason?" he says, stepping on the gas. Now we're taking the curves at over two
hundred miles per hour.

"Slow down!" I shout. "*Now* I'm frightened."

"I'm sorry, Anna, but we have to outrun him," Earl says.
"This car is made for speed."

"Didn't you also say it was a movie prop from thirty years
ago or something?"

"Well, yes," he concedes.

"And anyway, I've seen NASCAR races. I've seen these cars wipe out and go up in flames."

"Then how would you recommend we shake our friend off?" he says.

"I don't know. Do you have a gun?"

"You think I carry a gun with me in the glove compartment of my stock car, Anna? What kind of thug do you think I am?"

"I'm sorry," I say.

"But you have a point. I think I have a bazooka in the backseat," he says. "Let's trade places—you take the wheel."

We're going almost three hundred miles an hour down the highway, but we switch places without slowing down. It's only when I'm in the driver's seat that I remember something important. "I don't have a driver's license," I tell Earl.

"Don't worry," he says, leaning into the backseat and opening an oversized violin case. He pulls a bazooka out.

"I've never driven a car before, either," I protest. My foot is on the gas and I'm trying to steer. It's just enough like Super Mario Kart that I sort of have the hang of it.

"You're doing fine," Earl says, loading the bazooka.

"Thank God it's not a stick shift," I say. I've heard stories about stick shifts. While they might make for fun double entendres, I hear driving them can be a bitch.

Earl looks at me, confusion plastered all over his face. "It *is* a stick shift, Anna," he says.

Uh-oh.

"Don't worry, though," he says. "I'll just fire a warning shot at this guy; he'll back off, and hopefully you won't have to change speed. Okay?"

I nod, as the hills zip by us on the right . . . and a thousand-foot cliff looms to the left. *Gulp.*

Earl tries rolling down his window, but it's locked. "Can you turn the child lock off?" he asks me.

As I search the driver's-side door for the child lock, the PT Cruiser chasing us taps our bumper. I grab the steering wheel with both hands and start hyperventilating. "I can't do this," I say.

Earl grips my arm and gazes gazingly into my eyes with his steely gray eyes. Even in almost total darkness, they look as beautiful and luminescent as ever. What did I do to deserve this gorgeous man? "You can do this," he says. "Now unlock the windows and keep your eyes on the road and your foot on the gas pedal."

"Yes, Sir," I say, grinning. I find the child lock and flip it so that Earl can roll his window down.

He grins at me. "Let's show this SOB what happens when you ride Earl Grey's ass." He leans out the window and aims the bazooka at the PT Cruiser.

"Fire in the hole," he says, shooting the bazooka. All this talk about riding asses and firing in holes is turning me on. I can't wait until we get back to his penthouse . . .

The PT Cruiser explodes behind us in a fiery inferno that lights up the mountainside. *Woah.* Earl grabs the wheel and we trade places again. He slows the car and turns it around.

"I thought you were just firing a warning shot," I say.

"That was what I was trying to do," he says. "It was also my first time using a bazooka. My bad."

"Could anyone have survived that?" I ask.

He shakes his head. "I don't know, but we're going to find out."

Earl drives the car up to the edge of the wreckage, which is still blazing. He leaves the car idling with the headlights illuminating the crash site and steps out. I follow him.

There's a crumpled body on the ground crawling out of the twisted metal. Earl bends over and rolls the person onto their back. It's a bruised and bloodied elderly woman I instantly recognize as one of the door greeters from my Walmart store.

"Mother!" Earl says.

"Oh, my baby boy," she says weakly. She looks like hell, but that's to be expected since she just survived a car chase that ended in a bazooka blast.

"I thought you were dead," he says, cradling the woman in his arms.

"I faked my own death so you could never find me," she says. "I didn't want you to see your poor mother as a casino junkie. Even after I shot my blackjack dealer in the face and got clean, I knew that I could only complicate your life. After rehab, I applied for the only job an ex-addict who looks thirty years older than her driver's license can get in this country—"

"A Walmart greeter," I say.

"Exactly," she says, nodding. "I had written you off completely, Earl. Until last week, when you walked through the automatic doors and back into my life."

"At the Portland Walmart," he says.

"Yes. You didn't see me—no one looks at us greeters—but I immediately knew it was you. Your tousled hair, penetrating gray eyes, and long fingers haven't changed a bit since you were a baby."

He shakes his head in disbelief. "Why follow us, though? Why not try to contact me?"

"I wasn't sure you would want to talk to me," she says, hacking up a lung. Earl tosses it aside. "I wanted to know you were okay, though," his mother continues. "Stalking you seemed like the only reasonable option."

Like mother, like son . . .

"Now that I know you're alive, I'm not going let you leave me again," Earl says. "You won't die on me, dammit." He throws her over his shoulder and carries her to the stock car, then pops the trunk and dumps her body inside. Earl slams the trunk shut. "Let's ride."

We speed back down the highway toward Seattle in silence. What I wouldn't give to know what's going on inside his mind right now! He grits his teeth, but keeps his eyes on the road.

We pull up to the same hospital I was discharged from earlier, and Earl removes his mother from the trunk. He hoists her in the air and plops her down into a wheelchair once we're in the hospital waiting room. Earl's mother is pale and unconscious. And possibly not breathing.

"Is she going to be okay?" I ask Earl, who is texting on his BlackBerry.

"Dr. Drew will be here shortly," he says. "He'll know what to do."

"But I don't think she's breathing. Shouldn't we do the Heimlich maneuver or something?"

Earl looks at her lifeless body. "She doesn't look good, I'll give you that."

She pops her eyes open. "I never look good," she mutters.

"OMG," Earl says. "I thought I'd lost you again."

"I'll be fine," his mother says. "All I want is for you to be happy. You kids go and do whatever it is you were going to do."

"Are you sure?" Earl says. "We had some kinky sex stuff planned, but we can totally put that on hold."

His mother shakes her head. "Go do your thing. If twenty years of pumping quarters into slot machines didn't stop my heart, some little car crash isn't going to."

Earl kisses her forehead. "I'll be back to check up on you."

He takes me by the hand. As we're leaving the hospital, he stops in the doorway. "Thank you for everything," he says, placing a hand under my chin and raising my eyes to meet his. "I couldn't face my mother returning from the dead without you by my side."

Earl kisses me passionately. He's so sweet that I temporarily forget he's taking me back to his penthouse to show me just how sadistic he can be. For the moment, though, I enjoy his lips on mine.

Chapter Twenty-six

BEND OVER THE BED," Earl commands. He has changed from his NASCAR jumpsuit into a black leather vest and flannel kilt. Rubber prosthetics are attached to his ears so that they appear pointed. I am only to address him as the Elfin Warlord Sliverin, he says. I am completely naked except for a pair of faery wings tied around my back. My faery princess name is Labiamajora.

"Stay," he says. Earl leaves me bent over the edge of the waterbed. I watch the green lava hypnotically separate and clump back together in the lava lamp beside the bed. When I hear him return, there's a faint jingling. What is he planning? My inner guidette hides in her tanning bed.

"The Elf Council has found you guilty of stealing mead from our supply shed," Earl says. "How do you plead?"

"Guilty," I say, exactly as he instructed me prior to our "scene." I try to turn my head to see what he's going to hit me with, but he orders me to keep my face down and eyes shut.

"I'm going to roll a standard D-twenty to determine how many times to paddle you as punishment for your crimes against Elfkind," he says. I hear him roll the twenty-sided die on the nightstand.

"Nineteen," he says.

Gulp.

"After each blow, you are to count out loud. Do you understand?"

I nod. I feel him rub my butt cheeks with his palms, massaging them. It feels good. Why can't we just give each other massages? I close my eyes and bite my lip, ready for the beating to commence.

WHAP! I feel the full force of a flat object paddle my left buttock. The telltale jangling gives it away: he's using his tambourine. I was expecting to scream in pain, but I have skinny jeans that hurt my ass worse.

"Count!" he yells.

"Wait, Slytherin," I say. "Time-out."

"Time-out?"

"Am I supposed to count once for each butt cheek, or does it count as one time for the pair?"

"I hadn't thought of that," he admits. "How about we count each cheek separately. And it's *Sliverin*, not *Slytherin*."

"Okay," I say. "One!" I almost add, "ha ha ha," like the Count from *Sesame Street*, but I'm somehow able to contain myself.

"Good girl, Labiamajora," Earl says. "The Elf Council will be pleased that you have accepted your punishment so eagerly."

He swats me with the tambourine again. "Two!" I shout. It takes all my power not to giggle, as I just can't get the *Sesame Street* Count out of my head.

Earl hits me a third time and I yell, "Three!" I finally let out a small giggle. Maybe if he was actually hurting me I would be able to contain myself. My butt barely even stings.

He ignores the laugh and hits me again. "Four!" I shout, immediately breaking down into uncontrolled laughter.

He hits me again, and again, and again. Every time he strikes my ass with the tambourine, I count out loud. And laugh. My voice gets weaker, and by the time we reach "seventeen," I'm ready to tap out. I can't take anymore. The pain from laughing is giving my abs a real workout.

"Count, Labiamajora," he says sternly.

It takes all my willpower to gather myself. "Seventeen," I say. I think I've finally contained my laughter, until a loud snort escapes through my nose.

"You think this is funny?" he says, paddling me again.

I'm laughing so hard that tears are running down my face now.

"Count!" he yells.

"I can't," I say weakly.

"Surely you know what number comes after seventeen? Or did they not teach you that at faery boarding school?"

"Yes," I say, whimpering.

"'Yes' isn't a number," he says, smacking me again.

"Eighteen!" I scream. "Nineteen!" My legs buckle and I fall onto the floor in a fit of laughter.

When my breathing finally returns to normal, I pull myself up. Earl is lying on the waterbed, his head buried in his forearms. I sit down next to him and put an arm on his back.

"Get away from me!" he says petulantly.

"I'm sorry," I say. "I started thinking about the Count from *Sesame Street*, and then the tambourine was making that silly jangling noise, and you're wearing those pointy ears, and . . . I couldn't help myself."

He lifts his head and stares at me with his gray eyes. "You think all of this is funny," he says, waving a hand around the Dorm Room of Doom.

"You want me to be honest, I'll be honest," I say. "You act like there's something wrong with you, like everything you enjoy is embarrassing or scary. News flash, Mr. Grey: This isn't 1950 or whatever. Your sexual tastes aren't as shocking or as deviant as you think. Neither is anything else you like. Maybe if you didn't take your fifty shames so seriously, I wouldn't be so compelled to laugh at them."

"I've already told you: I can't think of myself as 'normal.' This is all part of the identity I've built for myself. It's how I survived my tumultuous upbringing. It's how I survive day to day," he says.

I sigh. If I move in with him, and admit my feelings, and have his baby (oops, keep forgetting about that!), I will have no choice but to submit to him and put up with this perpetual pity party of his. You can't separate Earl Grey from his fifty shames. Why can't I fall in love with someone relatively normal, like my ethnic friend, the brony Jin?

"I can't handle this anymore," I say, fleeing from the Dorm Room of Doom.

"Anna!" Earl yells. He doesn't chase me down. I think this is what he wanted anyway: to scare me away. *Well, congrats.*

I call my mother from the Starbucks across the street. She's still in town, and agrees to pick me up at once. After I hang up the phone, I realize I'm still naked except for the faery wings. Oh well—my mother the nudist won't mind. The other customers in Starbucks aren't quite as enlightened.

"What, like none of you have seen a naked faery before?" I shout.

A dozen people, men and women, shake their heads. "Not in Starbucks," a teenage boy working as a barista says. "It's the juxtaposition of the naked female body with the mundane, sanitized setting of a chain coffee shop that makes it exciting. Plus the wings are just weird."

"Get over it," I say.

Then I remember something Kathleen told me once that should distract the gawkers. "The Starbucks logo used to feature a topless mermaid," I say. "Go stare at her double lattes."

Everyone pulls out their iPhones and Androids and whatever the hell smartphones they have these days and begins googling images of the topless mermaid. When my mother pulls up out front, I slip out of the coffee shop unnoticed; everyone is too busy wanking to the old Starbucks logo. Thank God they changed the logo—there are enough bathroom masturbators at Starbucks as it is.

Chapter Twenty-seven

I

T'S BEEN A WEEK since I left Earl Grey, and he hasn't
tried to contact me. I'm staying at my dad's house in
Portland. I didn't consider going back to the duplex I share
with Kathleen, not even for a second—she's probably still
mad at me. Plus, the entire place is undoubtedly still under
surveillance by Earl Grey, billionaire stalker extraordinaire.

My father is on my case about getting a job. I got so
wrapped up in my new life with Earl Grey that I forgot I
even worked at Walmart. Of course they would take me back
in a heartbeat—Earl Grey would make them, or else he'd
fire my boss or liquidate the company or something. I can't
see myself returning to Walmart, though. I never liked it
that much, and I'm eager to start a new chapter in my life. I
applied for a job at Amazon, a local Seattle publishing
company. They advertised a few openings in their warehouse, which sounds like a great entry-level position in the
book industry. If I get the job, I might be able to work my
way up to editor in a few years.

I'm sleeping in my old bedroom for the first time since I
moved in with my mother after my parents' divorce. The
room is exactly how I left it, right down to the stuffed animals and N*SYNC poster. It's a peaceful environment, a

return to the womb of sorts, but my mind won't stop racing. My father is at work, and I'm lying on my bed fully
clothed and trying to catnap. I close my eyes. My thoughts
invariably turn to Earl Grey. Would our life together really
be so bad? No matter how hard I try to be angry with him,
my body responds with increasing desire . . .

I unbutton the top two buttons of my blouse. This gives
me just enough room to slip a hand inside my shirt. I slide
my fingers between my bra and left breast. I trace the edges
of my areola before giving my hard nub a firm pinch. I
imagine Earl Grey, my handsome knight in shining armor,
knocking on the bedroom door and asking for a small fa-
vor. *If you don't mind.* (I don't.) He shuts the door behind
him. I drop to my knees and grab hungrily at his belt, rip-
ping it open like I'm tearing the bow off the greatest
Christmas present ever. I unzip his slacks . . .

I unbutton my own jeans just enough to slip my hand
down the front. I let out a slight moan. I can't believe I've
never done this before!

When I wake up, it's half past nine according to the clock
on the nightstand. I'm still on the bed, half in and half out
of my clothes. Damn—I must have been exhausted. All I've
been doing for the past week is sleeping and eating and
watching TV with my dad. I don't remember completing my
solo session; thank God I was alone! What if I had fallen
asleep with Earl Grey going down on me in his Dorm Room

of Doom? How would he have "punished" me? I button my jeans and sit up on the bed.

I switch the lamp on. The iPad Earl gave me is sitting on the nightstand. I haven't touched it in a week, but since Earl hasn't tried calling me, I doubt he has e-mailed me. Still, I turn it on out of curiosity and find an e-mail. From him.

From: Earl Grey <earlgrey50@hotmail.com>
Subject: Have a Nice Life
Date: June 6 8:39 AM
To: Anna Steal <annasteal@hotmail.com>

Dear Miss Steal—

It's been a week since you left me, and I still cannot get over the heartache. You saw me at my most sadistic and most embarrassing, and, as I predicted, I'm one shame too screwed up for you. If we can't be together, what do I have to live for? A lifetime of buying anything and everything I want with my vast fortune? None of it matters. The only thing I want is you.

Oh, and the latest Apple products. So I guess I want two things in life: you, and the latest Apple products.

And a Guns N' Roses reunion album. So, that's three things: you, the latest Apple products, and a Guns N' Roses reunion album.

No, take off the one about Guns N' Roses. Their last few records together were just okay, and Axl and Slash's solo projects have been Crap City, where the hooks are gone and the licks are shitty. I think that was just nostalgia talking. So, the only things I want in life are you and the latest Apple products.

Earl Grey
CEO, The Earl Grey Corporation

_____

I tap out a response to him:

From: Anna Steal <annasteal@hotmail.com>
Subject: RE: Have a Nice Life
Date: June 6 9:56 PM
To: Earl Grey <earlgrey50@hotmail.com>

Mr. Grey—

I touched myself today for the first time. I thought of you.
I thought of us . . .

It's a crazy world we live in. This world is fifty times more
screwed up than you will ever be. Don't do anything
stupid. If we're meant to be together, it will happen. If it's
not meant to be, then can either of us blame the other?

Anna

P.S. I'm preggers.

Immediately after I tap "send," there's a knock at the window. I set the iPad down, cross the room, and throw open the curtains. Instead of Earl Grey, it's Jin.

"Can I come in?" he says, his voice muffled through the glass. He's wearing tight cutoff jean shorts and seems to have lost his shirt. His muscles ripple in the moonlight. *Oh my.*

Chapter Twenty-eight

I OPEN THE GLASS WINDOW, but that still leaves the screen. Jin waits at my window ledge patiently, standing on a ladder that he's leaned up against our house so he can reach my second-floor window. Unfortunately, no matter how hard I try to open it, the screen is stuck.

"Can you use the door?" I ask him.

He mutters something under his breath and backs down the ladder. Thirty seconds later, I hear him coming up the steps inside the house. I unlock the bedroom door and greet him with an awkward hug.

"Hey, you," I say.

"Hey, you too," Jin says.

We sit down on the bed at arm's length from each other. I don't want him to get the wrong idea—my relationship with Earl Grey might be on shaky ground, but it doesn't mean my sperm bank is accepting donations.

"I heard you were back in town," Jin says.

"You heard correctly," I say.

"I saw the accident on the news. Kathleen and I thought you were dead for sure."

"I'm not," I say.

"Obvs," Jin says.

"So you did hear about the crash, then. I was beginning to wonder . . ."

"You were beginning to wonder? Why? Because we didn't visit you when you were in the hospital? I tried to, believe me. The security was so tight there because of that celebrity doctor treating you that they were only letting in immediate family to see you."

And Earl Grey, my inner guidette whispers. "How are things going with your bronies?"

"I wasn't sure how they would react after I succumbed to my anger at Eclipse and fought with your boyfriend, but they've been incredibly cool and supportive. I've learned that every brony struggles with feelings like anger. It's incredibly helpful to talk through those feelings with my bronies."

"And your forum moderator job at PonyExpression .net?"

"It's all good. It's the best job I've ever had—and since I have a million dollars now, I don't have to worry about getting some boring 'real' job. I've even got a small Australian vanity press interested in publishing my pony fan fiction."

"That's fantastic, Jin. I always believed in you," I say. "How are your testicles?"

"The one I have left is fine," he says.

The tone of his voice makes it sound like a sore subject, so I quickly change the topic. "How is Kathleen?"

"After she drove us into the Pacific Ocean, she decided to clean herself up. She knew she had a problem for a long time, but that accident was what finally drove her over the

edge. So to speak. I dropped her off at an inpatient treat-
ment center. She'll stay there until she's thirty days sober
and then move to a halfway house, but so far so good."

"Is she still a B?" I ask.

"Of course. She's still Kathleen," Jin says, grinning.
"She'd like for you to visit her, though. She wants to know
if you're still planning to move to Seattle with her, or what
your plans are. Do you even know?"

"The future is kind of up in the air," I say. "I applied for
a job in Seattle, but who knows if I'll get it."

"You're living her dream, you know," he says. "Dating a
boardroom hottie, hanging out in Seattle . . ."

I shake my head. "She shouldn't take it so personally."

"Are you still seeing him?"

"Who?"

"C'mon, Anna. How long have we been friends? Four
years? You can tell me anything."

"I'm not sure if Earl Grey and I are still together or not,"
I say. "Things are complicated."

Jin shakes his head. "Why can't love be easy?"

"Because nothing good ever comes easily," I say.

Jin puts a hand on my knee. "I come easily."

I try to imagine what life would be like if I took him up
on his offer. We've always been close friends. If we took
things to the "next level," how would our friendship
change? I have to admit that our friendship has already
changed as a result of Earl Grey, who brought all the sexual
tension that had been simmering for years between me and
Jin to the surface. And now that tension is simmering in

Jin's cutoff jean shorts. It would be so easy to just lean over, unbutton his shorts, and—

There's a knock at the door. *Oh no!* Is it Earl Grey?

Nope. My dad opens the door. Jin takes his hand off me.

"Oh, sorry—didn't know you had company," my dad says.

"This is Jin," I say. "He's a brony."

Jin shakes my father's hand.

"This isn't the feller who landed you in the hospital, is it?"

I shake my head. "No, Dad. That was Earl Grey."

"You kids grow up so fast," my dad says. "One minute, you're watching *Barney* and the *Teletubbies*. The next, you're being fingered by some brony. You kids have fun. I'm taking a couple of Ambien and hitting the hay. Don't stay up too late."

He shuts the door and I'm alone again. With Jin.

"I'm sorry," I say. "He tends to say really inappropriate things."

Jin laughs. "Now I see where you get it from."

Suddenly, Earl Grey emerges from beneath the bed!

Chapter Twenty-nine

HELLO, ANNA," Earl says, dusting himself off. He's wearing his suit and smiley-face tie again. I remember the tie well . . .

I stand up to distance myself from Jin. "Whatever you think was happening, it wasn't," I say.

"What if I think nothing was happening? Does that mean something was happening?" Earl says.

"I'm confused," I say.

"What else is new?" Jin mutters.

"Don't worry," Earl says to me. "Someone's about to get fingered in this room, and it isn't you."

"Did you just threaten to finger me?" Jin says, standing up. His muscles ripple angrily.

Oh no. Not another fight. Jin will never forgive himself if he lets his anger overtake him again. Plus he only has one testicle left. "Both of you—STOP!" I shout.

They look at me. "Stay out of this, Anna," they say in unison.

"Jinx," Earl says.

Jin swears silently under his breath. If he talks now, Earl can hit him. It's the jinx code.

I shake my head. "Un-jinx him, Earl. Don't you get it? If you fight each other over me, you both lose."

"Just tell me one thing, Anna—is the baby mine . . . or his?" Earl says.

Jin looks at me. He is heartbroken. "You have a bun in the oven, Anna?"

Earl raises a fist to hit Jin in the arm for breaking the jinx code. I grab his hand and prevent him from punching Jin. "You know I can't bake," I say.

"I was talking about you being knocked up," Jin says.

"Oh. That. I'm sorry I didn't tell you sooner," I say.

Jin shakes his head. "You're lying," he says.

"No," I say. "I'm carrying Earl's baby."

"You're no better than those pregnant sixteen-year-olds on MTV that Kathleen is obsessed with," he says.

"Take that back," I say. "I'm not sixteen. And I would never be on a reality TV show."

"Sounds kind of funny coming from a girl whose personal physician is Dr. Drew," Jin says. "Face it, Anna: you've changed."

"Have I? Or have I just grown up?"

Jin frowns. "This isn't how things are supposed to end. You know it." He might be upset, but at least his anger seems to have dissipated.

"I'm sorry, Jin," I say. "Maybe you can fall in love with the baby when he grows up?"

Earl scowls at me.

"Or maybe not," I say. "Look, the point is, there are plenty of ponies in the sea."

"Yeah, and they're called 'seahorses,'" Jin says, sulking.

"You know what I mean," I say. "Being a friend sometimes means you have to let your friends go."

Jin sighs. "You're right. Instead of being happy for you, I've been jealous. I wish I could control my emotions better. If I've learned anything, though, it's that being a brony is a continual journey and not a destination. I'm going to leave now, and I'm not sure when we'll see each other again. But I sincerely hope you and Earl Grey are happy together."

"Thank you. That means a lot to me," I say, opening my arms and embracing Jin in a long hug. I feel his hands creeping down my back and when they're almost at my butt Earl clears his throat.

"Goodbye, Anna," Jin says, letting go of me.

"Goodbye, Jin," I say. "And good luck."

Jin and Earl stand face-to-face again. Earl taps him playfully on his naked bicep. "That's for breaking the jinx code," Earl says.

"Be good to her," Jin says, extending an open hand.

Earl shakes it. "I will be."

Jin tries to open the window screen but it won't budge. "You weren't kidding about it being stuck," he says. He walks out the door instead, shutting it behind him.

Earl embraces me. "When I got your e-mail, I was worried about who the father was. I'm just glad the kid won't have a dad who collects plastic toy ponies."

"I think Jin is still finding himself. He has his own journey ahead," I say. "Thank you for not having him brutally murdered or something."

"I was never too worried that he could take you from me. Remind me later to cancel the hit I put out on him, though," Earl says, confidently placing a hand on my shoulder. I melt at his touch. My inner guidette spins in circles until she collapses in a dizzy heap.

"I applied for a new job this week," I say, trying to avoid the baby in the room.

"At Amazon," he says.

"How did you know? Don't tell me you bought them too . . ."

Earl laughs. "I already owned them. Don't worry, though—I won't interfere with your career."

"Thanks. That means a lot to me," I say. "I've also been meaning to ask how your mother is."

"Physically? She's alive, which is more than you can say about most Walmart greeters," he says. "Emotionally? We've got a long road ahead of us to patch up our relationship."

There's an awkward pause. He could very well be talking about *our* relationship.

"I'm sorry I got pregnant," I say.

Earl gazes into my eyes. "It's more than likely my own fault, Anna," he says.

"What do you mean?"

"Remember when I said my condoms are tailored?" he says.

I nod.

"Here's the thing," he continues. "Apparently hemming a condom for a better fit isn't such a smart idea. The sperm can swim right through the stitched seams."

"Huh," I say.

I lay my head on Earl's chest and immediately start sobbing.

"What's wrong?" he asks.

I stare into his gazing gray eyes. "What's wrong? Don't you get it? I'm in love with you," I say. The secret's out.

Earl Grey's face lights up with joy. I've never seen him so happy, except for maybe when he's emulating his hero, Tom Cruise.

"I'm in love with you, Earl Grey," I repeat. "When I ran out of your penthouse, I was confused. I've since realized that love is a bumpy ride; every rose has its thorns. I hope you'll take me back."

"Of course I will," he says. "I was worried *you* wouldn't take *me* back. I should have cut you some slack when you laughed at our role-playing session—at least you're open to new things. I know what a sadistic prick I can be, Anna. It can't be easy to deal with the moody Earl Grey, but you seem to handle me better than any woman I've been with. You're not afraid of my fifty shames, and you've taught me that I shouldn't be either. Baby, I was born this way."

I laugh. "I didn't know you were a Lady Gaga fan! I love her. It sounds like you and I were meant for each other."

"I'm not sure who that is, but speaking of being meant for each other . . ." Earl gets down on one knee and produces a jewelry box from his pocket. "Remember when I said I wasn't the kind of guy who could see himself with a girlfriend?"

I roll my eyes. *How could I forget?*

"While I stand by that statement," he says, "I *can* see myself as the kind of guy who has a wife."

"I think that kind of guy is called a 'husband,'" I offer.

Earl smiles and opens the jewelry box, revealing a gold engagement ring topped with a gleaming rock. "Anna Steal . . . will you marry me?"

"Yes! Yes, yes, yes!" I say, unable to contain myself. Literally, I am unable to contain myself, as urine trickles down my leg.

I remove the ring from the box and slide it on my finger. Upon closer inspection, the stone is actually a diamond-studded twenty-sided die. *Oh my.* The ring is so heavy I can barely lift my hand. My inner guidette does a fist pump. I want to spend the rest of my life with this amazing, rich, attractive, rich man. "This calls for a celebration," I say.

"I think I know what you mean," he says, embracing me and lowering me onto the bed.

"Hold on," I say. "Did you just hear something? In the closet . . ."

Earl marches over to the closet and throws the door open.

"Dr. Drew!" he screams.

The doctor stumbles out of the closet. "Sorry, I was just, ah . . . leaving." Dr. Drew scampers out of the room. As he barrels down the stairs, I hear him trip and roll the rest of the way to the bottom. Dr. Drew screams for help, something about a bone showing.

"Should we go check on him?" Earl asks, peering out the door.

"No," I say. "He's a doctor—he can heal himself."

Earl closes the door. "I believe we were getting ready to celebrate," he says, removing his jacket and tossing it across the room. He loosens his tie. "Care to join me?"

Now it's my turn to smirk. "Actually, there's something *I* want to try, for a change," I say, propping my head up on a teddy bear. "Leave the tie on, and take off your pants."

"Yes, Miss Steal," he says, grinning wickedly. He slips out of his gray dress pants and silver thong, revealing his slender, muscular legs. His manhood, jutting out from underneath his dress shirt, is primed and ready to go.

"Get your ass over here," I order him. I kind of like being in charge.

He does as he's told, and stops beside the bed. "What exactly did you have in mind, Miss Steal?"

"My fiancé's name is Earl effing Grey. If you don't teabag me right this second, I'm calling bullshit."

He shakes his head. "It's a shame we didn't do this sooner. I love you, baby," he says, straddling me on the bed.

"And I love you," I say.

He dips his sack into my open mouth. As I taste his expensive coconut-lime body wash, any remaining uncertainty over our future together fades. I love him: the father of my child, my future husband, my lover, my partner in kink, my Maverick . . . my beloved Edward Cullen. I mean, "Earl Grey."

Epilogue

"**M**ISS STEAL, you've been in labor for sixty-five hours now. The baby is in trouble. We have no choice but to do a C-section," the obstetrician says.

"Then do it, goddammit," Earl says. He has been here in the hospital, holding my hand throughout the entire ordeal. Carrying his baby to full term was painful enough, what with all its sadistic behavior in the womb, but the past sixty-five hours have been even more painful. The nurses can't pump enough painkillers into my system to stem the pain.

I squeeze Earl's hand. "It's . . . going . . . to be okay," I mutter. I am exhausted and need to rest, but I need to be strong. For our baby boy.

"Do we have your consent, Miss Steal?"

"Okay," I hear myself say. My voice sounds like it's coming from another dimension.

"Excellent," the obstetrician says. "This will all be over soon." She turns to a nurse and asks for the anesthesiologist, and then orders another nurse to wheel my bed into the operating room.

Everything happens so fast. We are whisked down a hallway, through another corridor, and into the OR. Earl, who is wearing scrubs over his suit, follows me, holding my hand every step of the way.

The next twenty minutes are a blur of doctors, nurses, and epidurals. I close my eyes, and can't feel anything. Thank God. I turn my head to Earl, and he smiles weakly. I feel myself slipping in and out of consciousness, but perk up when the obstetrician finally says the magic words: "Here's your son."

Earl is holding the newborn swaddled in a blanket. The baby's face is wrinkled, and his dark hair is matted down, but he's alive. And cute. His eyes are closed and he looks so peaceful. Chris Grey. Our baby.

Baby Chris's eyes open. They're gray just like his father's. Baby Chris smiles wickedly, and flashes his pointed vampire teeth. Wait—his what?!

I look up at Earl, who smiles and flashes his own pointed fangs. "I guess there's something we need to talk about," he says. The baby gazes at me, and I gaze at him, and then Earl gazes at me, and then we all take turns gazing at each other gazingly.

"Earl Grey & Anna Steal Married in Seattle"

A *BOARDROOM HOTTIES* EXCLUSIVE BY KATHLEEN KRAVEN

Three months after the birth of their first child, the Earl Grey Corporation's resident hottie Earl Grey and his fiancée, Amazon warehouse employee Anna Steal, have tied the knot. The couple was married in a hush-hush ceremony in Seattle's newly renovated Space Needle this April—and *Boardroom Hotties* was there with the exclusive!

Earl, 28, and Anna, 22, began dating nearly a year ago and caused an uproar when they "came out" in public at Earl's drunk diving charity ball. It also caused a stir around the *Boardroom Hotties* office, mainly because we had all assumed the mysterious Earl Grey batted for the other team. Not so!

Longtime *Boardroom Hotties* readers may remember Earl and Anna's close call last year, when their helicopter crashed into the Space Needle. Thankfully, Earl escaped without a scratch on his gorgeous face. Anna's injuries were more severe, but she recovered quickly thanks to celebrity doctor Drew Pinsky. Thirty-two tourists lost their lives in the accident, which totaled the historic landmark. Earl financed reconstruction of the towering structure, and the Space Needle now stands over 1,800 feet tall—nearly three times its previous height. Word on the street is that its new distinctive pinkish hue and "veiny" appearance are modeled after Earl's own "space needle." This reporter was unable to confirm the likeness, unfortunately.

The wedding ceremony was attended by close friends and family only. The groom's side of the aisle was packed with local celebrities, including Earl's adoptive father (and 1986 *Boardroom Hottie* of the Month) Bill Gates. The bride's nudist mother and stepfather made for some interesting family portraits!

The bride wore a tasteful white Louis Vuitton for Target bridal gown designed specifically for the occasion; the groom wore Tom Ford (literally—he draped the designer over his shoulders). Standing up for the couple were this reporter (as the maid of honor, celebrating eleven months of sobriety) and best man Tom Cruise. The ceremony was officiated by the Reverend Brent Spiner.

The happy newlyweds will be honeymooning with their infant son at Triassic Safari, Earl's private dinosaur park in Hawaii that he totally thought of way before Michael Crichton wrote *Jurassic Park*.

Earl Grey's Fifty Shames

The Complete, Unexpurgated List

1. Shopping at Walmart on Saturdays

2. Bondage with handcuffs

3. Plays BDSM (Bards, Dragons, Sorcery, and Magick)

4. Mancrush on Tom Cruise, even after all the Scientology/ Katie Holmes BS

5. Spanking

6. Actually likes the taste of Bud Light

7. Whipping

8. Flogging

9. Cried when Oprah went off the air, but never found the time to watch her cable channel

10. Caning

11. Backdoor sex

12. Prefers Jay Leno over David Letterman

13. Teabagging

14. Nipple clamps

15. Doesn't understand why everyone hated the *Star Wars* prequels so much

16. Thought Jerry Seinfeld was the funniest part of *Seinfeld*

17. Bath & Body Works Signature Collection Coconut Lime Breeze body wash

18. Cock rings

19. Doesn't get *Mad Men*—like, at all

20. Uses a PC laptop with an Apple sticker covering the Dell logo

21. Steals Wi-Fi from neighbors

22. Finds it incredibly erotic when women pick their noses

23. Nickelback

24. Only flosses teeth the week before a scheduled dentist appointment

25. Watches *Titanic* at least once a year, and laughs every time when that guy hits the propeller

26. Team Jacob

27. Trolls Craigslist for dates

28. Wishes Katy Perry and Russell Brand would reunite, because they were so good together

29. Thought Heath Ledger was "just okay" as the Joker

30. Olive Garden is his favorite Italian restaurant

31. Bondage with rope

32. Pays women to live-action role play (LARP)

33. Never finished reading Ayn Rand's *Atlas Shrugged*

34. Watches professional wrestling religiously even though he knows it's not "real"

35. *Gossip Girl*

36. Can't remember the last time he trimmed his toenails

37. Makes frequent references to *Snakes on a Plane,* even though it wasn't even funny to do so when the movie was in theaters

38. Vibrators

39. Thinks Tim Burton is kind of overrated

40. Wishes everyone would just leave Kristen Stewart alone

41. Lesbian porn doesn't really do it for him

42. Can eat a pint of Ben & Jerry's in under half a minute

43. Thinks Jeff Foxworthy is hilarious

44. Snowballing

45. Thinks you just can't beat a good floral-print Hawaiian shirt

46. Kind of thought George W. Bush was decent as commander in chief

47. Butt plugs

48. *16 and Pregnant*

49. Pegging

50. Reads erotic romance novels

Fifty Shames in Space

Earl Grey bends me over the railing overlooking the vast, alien jungle and takes me from behind. In our rush to get busy, we have stripped off only the minimal amount of clothing necessary, and are making love with our pants around our ankles and the rest of our space clothing untouched. The twenty-pound jetpack is still strapped to my back; it takes an eternity to get completely out of our space battle gear, and neither of us can wait another ten minutes to get hot and heavy.

As we bone under Xenux's twin moons, I think about all that's happened since the birth of our son: the human-vampire war, the invading alien forces that exploded the sun, the fact that Jin and Kathleen finally found true love (with each other), and then, six months later, their breakup after Jin caught her making sandwiches with the Winklevoss twins.

The closer I get to climaxing, the more my nipples ache to be touched. Finally, it is too much to bear. I fumble with my top, in a desperate attempt to free my breasts as I ride Earl to my pleasurable destination. One touch is all it will take to send me over the edge. Earl, sensing what I'm trying to do, wraps an arm around me to cup my left breast—but his long fingers find the jetpack's emergency booster switch instead.

I am shot three hundred yards across the jungle, where I crash-land into a tree.

It is the best orgasm of my life.

When I trek back through the jungle and find Earl, there's not much left of him. The direct blast from my jetpack's single thruster cut him in half at the waist. My poor Earl Grey is now fifty shades of messed up . . .

———∽———

Does Earl Grey survive? Find out in *Fifty Shames in Space*, the thrilling sequel to *Fifty Shames of Earl Grey*. Twice the sex, twice the excitement, and twice the sex!

Acknowledgments

Thank you to Brandi Bowles and the fine folks at Foundry Literary + Media for believing in this project. Pony power!

Thank you to Brandy Rivers and the Gersh Agency for scouting locations for my luxury mansion in Beverly Hills.

Thank you to Renée Sedliar, Lissa Warren, Sean Maher, Kevin Hanover, John Radziewicz, Alex Camlin, and everyone at Da Capo Press and Perseus Books Group.

Thank you to Christine Marra and Marrathon Editorial Production Services for beating the manuscript into shape.

Thank you to Jennifer Sullivan, Hilary Rose, and the entire Tantor Audio team.

Thank you to the talented Allyson Ryan for bringing Anna Steal to life for the audiobook.

Thank you to my beta readers, Tiffany Reisz and Karen Stivali.

Thank you to the thousands of readers who followed this story through the first three chapters back when it was serialized on EvilReads.com as *Fifty-one Shades*. I wasn't lying when I said I would sell out, change the characters' names, and hide from y'all in my brand new McMansion. Good luck getting past my alligator-filled moat!

And, last but not least, thank you to Stephenie Meyer for the inspiration.

Index

About the Author

Fanny Merkin ~~hides from her fans~~ lives in a Beverly Hills mansion purchased using the embarrassingly large advance she received for *Fifty Shames of Earl Grey*. She is a former Walmart employee who writes under the pseudonym "Andrew Shaffer" for publications as diverse as *Mental Floss* and *Maxim*. Andrew Shaffer is the author of *Great Philosophers Who Failed at Love*. He reviews romance, erotica, and women's fiction for *RT Book Reviews* magazine.

50shames.com
ThisMerkinLife.com